HOOLIGAN

MAINSTREAM SPORT

HOOLIGAN

EDDY BRIMSON

MAINSTREAM
PUBLISHING

EDINBURGH AND LONDON

First published in Great Britain in 1998 by
MAINSTREAM PUBLISHING COMPANY (EDINBURGH) LTD
7 Albany Street
Edinburgh EH1 3UG

ISBN 1 84018 083 8

Reprinted 1998, 1999, 2000, 2001(twice)

Hooligan is purely a work of fiction. All the characters, incidents and events
in this novel are fictional.

A catalogue record for this book is available from the British Library

Typeset in Van Dijck MT
Printed and bound in Great Britain by Cox and Wyman Ltd

For Harriet, whose love, faith and encouragement made this book possible. For Arthur, for helping me concentrate. And for my family, my friends, and all those living in the real world. Keep happy and good luck.

1

Mozzer stood with his knob in his hand and sighed with relief as the golden liquid flowed out. As usual the drinking had started early, it was only 11 o'clock but already the lager had taken effect. God knows he needed this piss badly and to him the service station was the most welcome place on earth. He couldn't hold out until they reached the pub and so, reluctantly, the lads had agreed to pull in so that 'the lightweight' could relieve himself while they waited in the van in order to hurry him up. As far as they were concerned Mozzer was wasting valuable drinking time.

As Mozzer stared at the blue and white tiles in front of him he suddenly felt uneasy. Someone was watching him. Behind him at first, then at his side. He looked to his left and eyeballed a young lad, about 24 years old. He was white with black hair cut in that shite northern style, and he was dressed in expensive designer clothes. Over his shoulder he could see another lad, younger still but the same model, a casual. Both were staring straight at him, their eyes burning into his skin. Mozzer tried to focus back at the tiles in front of him as though nothing out of the ordinary was happening but inside his stomach was churning and his legs felt as if they had begun to turn to jelly. His mind was racing.

> *. . . Who the fuck? . . . I don't believe this, I can't get turned over with my dick hanging out . . . maybe I can stall them until . . . if only one of the fucking lads would turn up . . . maybe . . . shit . . . SHIT! . . .*

The older lad piped up. 'Where you from then, pal?' He was a Scouser. Mozzer hated Scousers. He said nothing. Holding his penis in his left hand he stared straight ahead as he gently slipped the right into his jacket pocket. The feel of the cold steel on his fingertips breathed hope back into his body. The Scouse was becoming agitated.

'I asked you a fucking question, twat. You're fucking London, ain't ya? A fucking Cockney wanker!' Mozzer's fingertips worked their way through the holes and gripped the weapon. Relief. The Scouser had missed his chance, taken far too long and now the knuckle-duster was loaded and ready. Mozzer pushed his penis back into his Armani boxers and turned to face the enemy. Both the Scousers took a small step back as a smile crept across Mozzer's face. His right arm shot out like a bullet, the cold steel smashing against the temple, ripping skin, cracking bone and sending blood splattering across the mirrors opposite as the Scouse fell to the floor, out cold. Mozzer then buried a size nine into the stomach of his victim just to make sure before turning on the younger lad. He had shit himself and backed off into the corner. Mozzer laughed as he closed in on his prey. *He* was in control now and was moving in for the kill.

'Yeah, I'm *fucking London*.' An insane grin spread across Mozzer's face as the lad fell to the floor and curled up in a ball waiting for the leather to hit home. Mozzer stood above the shaking youth. He reached in his pocket to search out two small business cards. First Mozzer studied the print as if to make sure, then flicked one of the cards at the shitter beneath him. On the white thick board, printed in bold blue letters were the words:

CONGRATULATIONS. YOU HAVE JUST MET THE CITY
BLUE ARMY . . . (THE CBA) . . . NOW FUCK OFF.

Mozzer mocked the youth below him and began to laugh. 'You wanker. You're not worth the polish off my fuckin' boot.' As he turned to leave, Mozzer dropped the other card on the motionless body of the other youth. 'Here, have one for your mate as well. Get him to give us a call when he's feeling a little better.' It landed in the pool of blood that was still working its way out of the open wound on the side of the Scouser's head. Stepping over the body Mozzer slowly made his way to the exit. He checked himself in the mirror before offering a final message to the startled onlookers. 'Safe journey, everyone.'

2

Mozzer explained the incident away as the Transit continued up the M1. Clarkie had wanted to go back and really finish the job. Everyone hated Scousers but Clarkie had more reason than most. The eight-inch scar across his left shoulder provided a constant reminder of a previous encounter a few years back when he had walked into the wrong pub and taken a good hiding. Some bastard had tried to slash his face with a Stanley knife but Clarkie had spotted it just in time and the thrust had caught his shoulder instead. The knife had been primed with two blades fixed either side of a matchstick in order to leave the nastiest scar possible. Clarkie had a habit of bringing his right arm up across his chest and rubbing the scar whenever the Scousers were mentioned and his voice would take on a more menacing tone.

Fuck knows why the Scousers were there anyway – *they* didn't have a game today. They must have been a couple of chancers who recognised the Londoner from a previous 'meeting'. Today, however, their luck had run out. One thing was for sure – the place would be crawling with Old Bill and this particular little mob didn't want a tug whilst on their way to a meaningless pre-season fixture against Mickey Mouse opposition. Mozzer had done a good enough job for the chancer to go back and inform his mates that the CBA were up for the coming season, while Clarkie was assured that he would get a pop at the Scousers at some other time during the coming months. Clarkie grumbled then finally stopped rubbing his scar.

Eighteen bodies in the back of the Transit, along with the empty cans and food packets made for an uncomfortable journey. Today they weren't looking for trouble, this was a pissheads' day out not a 'firm's outing'. And anyway most of Mozzer's top boys were still on holiday in Tenerife, drinking and shagging in the sun. He knew only too well that there would always be a few of the locals up for a bit of bovver, and that the CBA were expected to show. It was also possible that some of the larger clubs such as Forest, Leeds or Birmingham would turn up to do a bit of scouting, and if that was the case then things could turn out a little different. But unless it was right in their faces Mozzer's firm would leave it up to the 'Juniors' or the 'Under Fives' mob to sort out.

Mozzer took a good look around the contents of the van. Despite the lure of the sun, cheap beer and the birds of Tenerife he still had a few of the main troops on board. Clarkie was a top bloke, 37 years old and still in there when it counted. Two kids hadn't halted his activities and so his wife had left him. Nowadays he would take the girls on for the summer to give his 'ex' a break, then during the season he had them on the weekends the Blues were at home, dropping them off at their granny's for Saturday afternoon. The perfect football family, minus the wife and the kids! He was a well-built bloke with close-cut hair to hide the receding hairline, and he would fight like a madman.

Chris and Shep were along for the ride as well as Ossie, Tony and Danny, five real diamonds. This lot had known each other since infant school and stuck together no matter what. They all attended the same boxing club when they were kids and Shep and Danny had gone on to box in the ABA Championships. They were always up for the crack, forever happy, but never mouthy. Every one was as hard as fuck, and if you took one of this lot on then you had to take on all five.

Mozzer loved to watch them in action and he was well chuffed that they were part of *his* firm.

The rest of the van was made up of lads from some of the other smaller mobs that followed the club. They came from towns such as Woking, Hemel Hempstead and Bromley. Most of the time these lads did their own business, building their own reputations. But for the big games they all came together under the banner that was City FC. Today they came together for the usual pre-season shant. For games like these Mozzer would also invite a few of the Juniors along. He knew that within their ranks lay the future reputation of the club and it was important that they felt wanted by the older lads, just as Mozzer had been made to feel wanted when he was much younger. Some had already proved their worth at various rows from the previous season and were nearly ready to make the step up from the younger mobs and join the CBA. Camden was one such lad. At just 19 he was not much to look at. A slim, almost skinny lad, he stood at just five foot seven but had one redeeming feature – bottle. Mozzer had seen him in action many times and knew that he would also use any weapon he could get his hands on. That combination made him dangerous, just what Mozzer required. His dad, Frank, was also in the van and was proud that his lad was keeping up the family tradition for terrace warfare. Mozzer loved the old man but by now Frank was well past his sell-by date as far as fighting was concerned. These days he just lived for the piss-up and the odd day out with the lads.

Mozzer's mobile phone rang. 'Hello.'

'Mozzer?' The voice was northern, Yorkshire.

'Yeah. Who's that?'

'It's Terry, mate, Sheffield United Terry. How's it going?'

Mozzer's reply sounded full of surprise. 'Hello, my son. Yeah, everything's lovely, mate.'

Mozzer had first met Terry during an arranged off at a service station involving the CBA and Newcastle's firm two seasons back. Terry was United's main man and had gone to see how both firms handled themselves after being tipped off about the row by another City mate of his who lived in the Steel City. Terry was impressed by what he had seen as both mobs defended their side of the service station. The bridge across the motorway was all that separated them and the place had become a real battle ground. To the passing motorists below it must have looked like World War Three had broken out and four people had been stabbed before the police finally put in a show. There was to be no let-up as both firms started to cross the carriageways in their attempts to reach each other. It had been a mental row and Terry was glad that on that occasion he had only been an interested spectator.

Terry was introduced to Mozzer once the fight was over and the two lads had hit it off straight away. United and City had one thing in common – both had been targeted by the Old Bill and both firms had come out on top as the infiltrators were soon discovered and fed false information. This information had wrecked all the court cases the filth had brought against those involved and made the Old Bill look complete idiots. Terry and Mozzer could have been sharing the same cell under different circumstances and the two had great respect and admiration for each other. The United firm had been particularly clever in tripping up the Old Bill and this had gained them respect from firms throughout the country. It also sent a message out to those in authority that they would never stop this form of Saturday afternoon entertainment.

The two lads would often meet to drink and swap the odd bit of information about who was planning what. Mozzer had helped Terry's lads avoid an ambush by Millwall fans at Moorgate Tube Station, and Terry would supply the Londoner with the names of any new pubs or clubs that the northern firms were starting to use. They would also let each other know about any up-and-coming firms that might require a visit before they got out of their depth and started playing with the big boys.

The conversation continued.

'You got a game today, Terry?'

'No, we played at Bury last night. Fucking useless bag o' shite. We're gonna struggle this year, I reckon,' Terry went on. 'Listen. You on your way up to Mansfield?'

'Yes, mate. In fact we're just turning off the motorway now. Why, do ya fancy coming down?'

'Aye, fucking great. Yeah, I'll come down. I need to see you as I've got some information your goin' t' love. Listen, don't go to Mansfield, it's a shit hole. Go to a village called New Houghton. I'll meet you in the Countryman pub, you can't miss it. I'll be 'bout an hour.'

'Nice one, I'll have one lined up for ya.'

The phone went dead and Mozzer directed the Transit off the A38.

3

Mozzer placed another pint on the table in front of Terry.

'So what's this news, then?'

'Well, word is out that the Leeds lads are going for it big time this season. All that shit with the police has fallen through, as ever, and your lot are their main target.'

Mozzer smiled as a few memories shot into his head.

'Leeds. It's about time those wankers got back on the case.' He sipped at his lager. 'What's it looking like, numbers-wise I mean?'

'Not bad, actually.' Terry took a long draw on his Embassy Number 1, paused, then blew the smoke skywards. 'Not bad at all. Y'see they've taken a few knocks recently. Middlesbrough and Man City both took the piss at their place last year. An' those Dundee lads that run with Stoke, well, they stopped off at one of their pubs last season an' gave them a right seeing to. A couple of the older lads took a serious hiding, ending up in hospital for a few days. One was in a pretty serious way. Since then there's been a lot a friction between the older lads and the young 'uns. You know the sort of thing – "It wouldn't have happened in our day" – that kind of bullshit. The older lads think everyone is taking liberties and they are right fucked off 'bout it. And so it's all back on, and big time by the looks of it.'

Mozzer quizzed the northerner further. 'So, what they got lined up then?'

'Well, in two weeks' time they play at Coventry an' rumour has it that on the way back they're hitting Stoke as pay-back for the Dundee off.'

Mozzer broke in. 'Fuck me, I'd love to watch that one. They'll do well to turn Stoke over on their own patch.' Mozzer's voice was tinged with surprise. The Stoke firm were more than up for it when his lads had met them twice in the cup the season before. He held his half-full glass to his mouth. 'They'll need big numbers to pull that off. Have the Stoke lads got wind of this yet?'

'No.' Again the Yorkshireman drew on his cigarette before stubbing it out in the ashtray. 'Not yet.' The pair laughed but Terry hadn't finished. 'But that's only the warm-up, Mozzer, lad. The week after they go to Highbury for the Arsenal match, and that's when they intend to hit you lot. Y'see they think you'll be tied up with the Newcastle lads at your place.' Terry paused once again to keep the Londoner in suspense.

Mozzer egged him on. 'Well, is that it?'

'Your place. The George pub in Ealing, that's the target.'

'Well, fuck me, they really do mean business, the bastards.' Mozzer sat back, smiling as his mind went into overdrive. Happily he went on. 'Terry, I owe you one, my son, big time. Those Yorkshire bastards won't know

14

what's hit 'em.' Suddenly he remembered Terry's birthplace and offered up an apology. 'Oh sorry, mate. No offence meant.'

Terry held his hand up and laughed. 'Don't worry about it, just get another pint in . . . ya Cockney cunt.'

4

All week Mozzer could think of nothing else.

. . . Leeds . . . Leeds . . . Leeds . . .

He had gone over and over every option.

. . . Should they wait for them to come down or see them off at King's Cross? . . . Would they come down early and hit on the Friday night or wait until late on the Saturday after everything else had calmed down? . . .

The CBA had tried that tactic at their place a few seasons back but had come unstuck. The Leeds firm had spotters trailing them all night and were ready when they went back for the kill. Mozzer had taken a fair hiding that night and would think twice before trying that move again.

. . . Would the Leeds lads use that same tactic? . . .

The firm relied on Mozzer to put every hit together. They never asked where he got his information from, or how he always knew what pub to hit. They didn't need to know, they just trusted him and he rarely let them down.

Mozzer needed to find out more. He picked up his mobile and dialled the number. The connection was made.

'Hello.'

'Hello, London calling.' Mozzer always used the same

words on such occasions. 'Can you tell me, are Leeds playing at Stoke in two weeks' time?'

'Eh, I'll try to find out. Ring back Monday at midday, I should have a better idea by then.'

'Sure, speak to you Monday then. Cheers.'

'Yeah, bye.'

5

Billy Davis hobbled back to his armchair, opened his tobacco tin and started to roll himself a huge joint. He had hoped that Mozzer would never ring again. The two had never spoken to each other face to face but Billy had seen the main man on many occasions, watching him from a distance.

Billy had once been a violent man himself. The past flooded his mind, memories of a time when he was one of the top boys in the firm, when he loved running with the mob. Away from football Billy Davis had made his money dealing in drugs and was a well-known face on the north-London scene. It was that world that had made the man a victim of a hit-and-run in which his pelvis and right hip had been shattered beyond repair, resulting in a permanent walking disability. The 'accident' came out of a bad deal in which Billy had become involved and it had left this once-fit young man a shadow of his former self. It had taken him a while to recover but during the six months he had spent in that hospital bed Billy had sworn to himself that he would track the driver down and have his revenge. That driver had ruined Billy's life and so, in return, Billy would take his. He often thought about just how easy it had been. To this day it still surprised him, one shot and it was over. He felt no remorse but this whole episode had forced Billy into moving away, leaving everything behind, including the firm. That was the reason why he found himself in a one-bedroom, ground-floor flat on a council estate in Nottingham.

Over the years Billy had started dealing again. It was the only way he knew of making a good living. He never liked the dole as he felt they could keep tabs on him, and that was something he definitely didn't need. Through his home-grown he had built himself a good reputation in the local pubs and it hadn't taken him long to establish a reliable circle of punters. But he missed the buzz of running with the firm. That was the one drug he craved more than any other.

After Billy was forced into doing a runner out of London he had kept in touch with just one member of the firm, Davy Philips. Davy was the top boy in those days and Billy's best mate. He had visited Billy every day in hospital and did as much for him as anyone could have done. Davy was Billy's only contact with his past and gradually, as Billy settled into his new surroundings, he would pick up information on the local firms and pass it back to Davy. This gave the CBA lads the edge on their rivals as they always knew where and when to hit. But more importantly, it kept Billy involved. It gave him the buzz, the fix he needed. As time went on Billy became more involved in scouting for the firm as the unsuspecting locals gave him all the information he needed. Once a few of the local lads had told him they suspected a mate of theirs of being a scout for the CBA firm because the Londoners always knew where to find their lads on match days. '*Really?*' was the surprised reply Billy always offered in return.

Unfortunately Davy had died three years back, but he had told Billy of the young lad that he saw as the next 'main man' ready to take over once he was past it all. That young lad was a certain Steven Morris, otherwise known as Mozzer. Davy had also given the youngster a number to call if anything unexpected ever happened to him, such as getting put away for a few years. That telephone number was the one Mozzer had just dialled and spoken to Billy Davis on.

No one had suspected that Davy would have had a heart attack, after all he was only 38 and as fit as a fiddle. Once the initial shock had died down Mozzer had rung the number and contact with Billy had remained ever since. Davy had told Mozzer that he could trust the contact 100 per cent. He wasn't wrong, Billy's information was always spot on.

Over the years, and through his drug dealing, Billy had come to know lads from all the top firms in the area. They loved to talk about their 'sport' with the old junkie, and he loved to listen. Since Davy's death the football drug had become even stronger. He wasn't content with passing the information on, setting up the rows and then reading about them in the local newspapers. Billy wanted to see it, video it. Once he was back home he would watch it over and over again, a link with his past and his dead best friend. Along with the drugs, the drink and hard-core Dutch porn movies, this was Billy's life.

But this life had caved in during the summer when he was raided by the Drugs Squad. Luckily he had been tipped off and removed his growing factory and ready-to-sell gear to a safe house a few days earlier, but on the morning of the raid a 'friend' had visited and offered Billy a bag of Ecstasy tablets. Pills weren't Billy's business. He had refused the offer, but less than half an hour later the police came crashing through the door and found the pills tucked down the back of the sofa, an obvious set-up that provided the Old Bill with enough evidence to send Billy away for five years, something he didn't need.

What Billy hadn't got rid of was his porn or, more importantly, his football violence videos. The filth couldn't believe what they had stumbled across, evidence that this crippled druggie was in some way playing a major part in organised football violence and they had him by the balls. The police, Billy, and his solicitor all knew the Ecstasy pills were a fit-up, and his brief had come to an agreement that the tablets would somehow become mislaid if Billy would assist in helping the filth nail the football firm. For Billy, it was the easiest way out. The raid had been a complete fuck-up as far as the Drugs Squad were concerned and so they wouldn't be troubling him again on that score, as that would only look like harassment. That was Billy's only stroke of good fortune as thankfully it enabled him to continue growing in relative safety. There was no other way out for Billy. Unless he played the game they would have him for dealing, and that would only be after they had tipped off the local football lads as to just who the scout was in their midst. Billy didn't fancy the porridge or having his other hip smashed and so the filth had what they treasure most of all — a grass.

6

The pub was heaving. Thursday nights were always a big night out for the lads as talk focused on Saturday's match and what might happen. Tonight had an added buzz. The troops had returned from Tenerife and were busy relaying stories of the fights, shags and piss-ups they had enjoyed during the previous two weeks. Clive had fallen in love with some sort from Essex and spoke of nothing else. What he didn't realise was that the rest of the lads thought she was a right boiler and that Dean had shagged her during the first week before Clive had even set eyes on her. Pinhead had a black eye following a run in with some Danish lads, and Rod had suffered from sunstroke and spent the last week tucked up in bed. For Mozzer, having the troops back was fantastic and The George pub was buzzing. Over in the corner he and Baggy were looking forward to meeting up once again with the Leeds mob.

'Meself, I think we should take it to them, Mozzer, hit 'em when they don't expect it.' Baggy was Mozzer's right-hand man. It was up to Mozzer to sort out the details but no decision was ever made without Baggy's final agreement. Baggy was a bright bloke. He ran his own courier company, was 34 years old, married and worth a small fortune. Away from the football he ran his life on the straight and narrow, never getting involved with any of the stolen gear or drugs that were always on offer around the firm. His wife Wendy was a real stunner and, all round, Baggy was one lucky bastard.

'Yeah, you're right. I've got people looking into it, but if they are going to hit the Stoke firm after a game at Coventry then they will have to pass through Crewe station.'

'It's the only way they can do it.' Baggy refreshed his throat with a quick drink. 'Let's have it at Crewe. We could get there before them cos we're at Villa that day.'

'That means Villa will have to wait though.'

'Fuck Villa, Mozzer. I really fancy havin' it away with Leeds again.'

'Yeah, you're right, Leeds at Crewe station.' Mozzer paused. 'That'll surprise the fuckers.'

'I hope so, because you know as well as I do, Leeds won't be easy.' The two smiled, tapped glasses and carried on drinking.

7

Billy woke the next morning and, as always, tended to his plants before anything else. What he couldn't risk was the police paying him another visit over the football. He needed the income the plants provided so he agreed that when he had some information he would go to them. He finished his breakfast then reluctantly picked up the phone.

'DI Young, Football Intelligence Unit, please.'

'May I ask who is calling?' came the reply.

'No.' Billy's retort was stern. 'It's private.'

'Hold the line, please, sir.' The receiver sent some annoying music into Billy's ear.

'Hello, DI Young speaking, how can I help you?'

'More like how can I help you.' Billy found talking to the copper disturbingly easy. 'It's Billy Davis here, I've got something for you. We need to meet.'

'Well, well, Mr Davis, good morning.' The DI sat up in his seat, surprised that the Cockney had called him without any prompting. 'Well, yes, this afternoon would be good for me. I could send you a car, is that OK?'

'Don't bother with the motor, but yes, this afternoon is all right. Two o'clock OK?'

'Fine, I'll look forward to seeing you then.' The other end of the line went dead as Billy refused to exchange pleasantries.

DI Young sat back in his chair thinking to himself . . . *Yes!* . . . He then smashed the desk with the palm of his hand and shot to his feet.

'Got the bastard.' He turned to the young officer sitting just yards away. 'Alan, get the lads together in the briefing room in half an hour, that was *our* Mr Davis on the phone.'

The young detective smiled back. 'Sure thing sir. Nice one.'

8

DI Young had been in the game a good few years and had quickly worked his way up the promotional ladder. Working with the Football Intelligence Unit was a natural progression as he had followed the game for as many years as he cared to remember. In his early youth he had even become involved in the odd skirmish but that was a long, long time ago and things had moved on a lot for him since those days. He had worked well at the local football clubs and had helped achieve good results at Forest and County by sorting out the ringleaders at both grounds. This had led to his latest promotion to Detective Inspector. Luckily for him Billy Davis had turned up after just three weeks at his new post, and a once-in-a-lifetime opportunity to smash the organised football firms had landed right in his lap.

His grey hair made him look older than his 45 years and middle age had definitely taken hold of his waistline, but his mind was fit. Billy had told him that he suffered a bad fall when he was a kid which had left him both physically and emotionally scarred. His disability had forced him into leaving home as soon as possible in order to start a new life away from his childhood memories of beatings and being bullied. He told DI Young about Davy, his best friend, and his involvement in the football violence. He told the DI of how Davy did everything he could for him and that in return he had become caught up in a seedy world that he couldn't escape from. The only real bit of truth Billy had offered to the DI was his link with the guy known as 'London'. DI Young had believed most of the story Billy had invented and almost felt sorry for the lonely southerner. But surely he knew the faces and their names. This Cockney must know where these hooligans worked, drank and lived. DI Young would work hard on Billy Davis for he held the key to the whole operation and this time the police were not going to fuck up.

9

Billy entered the interview room and sat down opposite the two policemen. DI Young started the conversation.

'Well, Mr Davis, it is good of you to come. Before we start would you like a tea or coffee?'

'No thanks,' replied Billy. 'But I'll ponce a fag, if that's OK?'

Detective Alan Lopes took a packet of Silk Cut from his pocket and offered one to Billy.

'You won't be putting anything stronger in that, will you, Mr Davis?'

Billy offered the detective a knowing smile. This reminder of the predicament he found himself in had set the 'good cop, bad cop' scenario from the start, something Billy had experienced many times during his life already.

'Well, I'll be brief, if you don't mind . . .' Billy had assumed that the police would have placed a tap on his phone soon after the bust and so he told them word-for-word about the conversation that had taken place with 'London' the day before.

'OK, Billy, that's good. But how will you find out the information this so-called "London" needs to set up this fight?' asked the DI.

'I'll just drop a few questions in my local tonight. Remember this weekend is the first full Saturday of the new season and so, for those involved in the violence, talk will be as much about that as the football. By Sunday lunchtime everyone in the pub will have some rumour they want to tell, I just have to sift the shit from the truth.'

Detective Lopes joined in. 'Listen, Davis, the DI here thinks you're just a sad old junkie. Me, I think you know a lot more than you're letting on.' He leaned forward, placing his face just inches from Billy's. 'This is no fucking game, Davis. Now why the fuck would they tell a sad little bastard like you all they get up to?'

'The local lads trust me. Simple.' Billy sat back in his chair unruffled. 'Anyway it ain't that difficult. People talk. Have you seen my video collection, Mr Lopes? Not bad for someone who knows nothing.'

The detective angrily spat the words out. 'It's Detective Lopes, you shit.'

Billy loved to call coppers 'Mr'. He knew it wound them up as it showed them no respect.

'You need me, *Mr* Lopes. I know you have me by the bollocks, but you need me.'

DI Young knew Billy was right and asked the detective to leave the room for a while so that they could all calm down. The two policemen had been playing a game with Billy, but to the surprise of the DI the Londoner had handled the situation better than he had expected. He realised Billy had been here before and that would make his job just that little bit harder.

'Billy, you said that the contact would call you back on Monday. Therefore I want to place a tap on your phone and record the conversation. I need you to sign some paperwork for me. OK?'

Suddenly Young's comments hit home with Billy. . . *Fuck it* . . . They hadn't tapped his phone after all, and this whole interrogation could have been avoided. The Londoner mentally kicked himself for being such a fool. Reluctantly he signed the forms and left the station. As he made his way home Billy thought about what Lopes had said. He was right, this wasn't a game. Billy had to start making plans of his own.

DI Young called Detective Lopes over to his desk. 'Well? First impressions?'

'It went well, sir. I am sure he knows a lot more than he is ever going to let on but with a bit of work we'll get enough out of him to crack it.'

'Do you think he's been here before?' asked the DI.

'Oh yes. He knew what was going on in there, all right. What we need to do is keep him thinking that we are a couple of idiots. That's when he'll start to trip up.'

'Good.' He paused to think things through. 'Right, the next move. As Davis said, it's the first day of the season tomorrow and City are at home. Me and you are off to London to take in the game and try to put some names to the faces in his videos. Get on the phone, liaise with the Met and find out who is in charge at their stadium. Then let them know we're coming. Oh and Alan? Good work in there. Well done.'

10

Mozzer never worked on Fridays at the best of times, but with the new season just 24 hours away this trip into the west end took on a new meaning. For someone with his gift of the gab, a job with a mobile telephone company was as easy as taking sweets from a child. As an area manager Mozzer often met his weekly objectives by Wednesday morning and from then on he would take things a little easier, slowing down for the weekend. Like most football hooligans Mozzer liked to wear the expensive designer clothing that was part and parcel of the movement. He didn't like to label himself a 'casual' as he had been part of the original movement of the '70s and '80s. He felt that these days too many jokers had jumped on the bandwagon. Back then if you wore the clothes it meant you were ready to fight. Today everyone wears the gear, even the birds, and so for Mozzer the label 'casual' was a blast from the past. But he still liked to dress to impress, and his pay packet allowed him the luxury of buying the very best that the London designer shops had to offer.

Dean and Pinhead were already waiting for him as he came out of Covent Garden tube station. They still had until Monday morning left of their holiday time and so they had arranged this joint shopping trip in the pub the night before. The two lads were still full of stories about Tenerife and it was all Mozzer could do to try and shut them up as they entered the Duffer of St George shop in Shorts Gardens. Mozzer loved this label. He liked the class of the clothes and the fact that the logo was not plastered all over every garment. He liked his label to be understated, not like all the foreign shit such as Tommy Hilfiger, YSL or Kappa. Mozzer didn't want to walk around wearing the stars and stripes of America, that was a wanker's thing to do. He was English, and an English label always got his vote.

After ten minutes browsing, Pinhead joined Mozzer and Dean downstairs. Dean was about to try on a new pair of blue strides but Pinhead had other plans.

'Oi, did you check the lad decked out in the Stone Island gear upstairs? Well, he is just about to lay out for that grey hooded Parka I've been after for the last three weeks.'

'Yeah, and?' replied Dean.

'Well, I don't know about you but the holiday skinted me out. That's 250 quid's worth of coat, that is, and I want it. If you help me jump him I'll bung you both 40 quid.'

Mozzer didn't need the money or the hassle but Dean wanted in.

'Is he on his own?' asked Mozzer.

'No, he has another bloke with him but he's nothing. Go on, Mozzer, it'll be a pushover.' Pinhead had a hint of desperation in his voice and so Mozzer gave in.

'Come on, then, Dean. I hate to see a grown lad beg.' The three lads made their exit, checking the opposition on the way out, and turned towards Neal Street. Mozzer and Dean stood together while Pinhead took up position some 20 yards away. After five minutes their target left the shop, turned towards them then walked on by and up towards Cambridge Circus. Pinhead gave the other two the nod and off they followed. This was Pinhead's shout and so it was down to him to call the shots. It was only on occasions such as these that Mozzer didn't mind playing foot soldier. The target crossed and headed up Old Compton Street.

Dean hated this part of London now. To him Soho used to provide a good night out for the lads. He remembered when this was the place to come and ogle the strippers and abuse the tarts, but not any more. Now Soho belonged to the gay community and Dean was not a fan. 'Look at all these fucking faggots, Mozzer. Don't it make you sick? Whenever I walk down here now my arse goes as tight as a gnat's chuff.'

'You don't want to walk down here like that, Dean. One of this lot will be up behind you like a rocket, you 'aving a nice tight little ring like that.' Mozzer took his hand out of his pocket and pinched Dean's arse.

'Fuck off, you cunt.' Dean shot forward as he swiped Mozzer's hand away. Mozzer laughed and in his best 'John Inman' shouted back, 'Oh don't be like that, honey, you didn't fight last night.' He then pouted his lips and blew Dean a kiss.

'You should be so fucking lucky.'

The lads' attention was drawn back to Pinhead. The geezer with the jacket and his pal had now moved off up Wardour

Street and Pinhead was ready to make his move. He jogged on past his target so that he could attack from the front, leaving Mozzer and Dean to steam in from the rear. As Pinhead scooted past his target Dean noticed the lad with the jacket clock him before turning to say something to his mate. The pair looked back over their shoulder to see Mozzer and Dean following on.

'The wanker, he's fucked it.'

Pinhead was totally unaware that he had been spotted. He stopped and then turned to head towards his prey. The lad holding the jacket handed the bag to his friend then pulled something from his pocket. Mozzer saw the glint of the metal.

'The fucker's got a blade.' Mozzer started to run towards them. 'Pinhead, leave it. The cunt's got a blade.'

Pinhead heard Mozzer's shout just in time, looked up and pulled his face away just as the metal flashed through the air, inches away from his cheek.

'COME ON, THEN. WHICH ONE OF YOU FUCKERS WANTS THIS, THEN?' The lad with the blade knew how to handle the weapon and had Pinhead trapped against the wall. He was shouting towards Dean. 'You want the fuckin' jacket, do ya?' He was pumped up on fear, excitement and adrenalin. 'Well, it'll look nice with a fucking ten-inch scar across your fucking face.'

Pinhead was shitting it. Mozzer moved forward.

'YOU CUT HIM, MATE, AND YOU'RE DEAD.' Mozzer had primed his trusty knuckle-duster and showed it to knife boy. 'Two can play that game, son.' Mozzer was playing a game of bottle but Pinhead wanted out.

'Fuck the jacket, Mozzer.' Pinhead tried to reason his way out. He turned to his attacker. 'Listen, mate, I fucked up, OK? Just move back and we'll fuck off out the way without anyone getting hurt.'

'FUCK YOU. NOT SO MOUTHY NOW, ARE YA?' He beckoned Pinhead forward. 'You wanted the jacket a minute ago. Come and get it.' The anger in his voice rose once more. 'COME ON.' Then he lunged forward. Once again the metal cut the air.

Pinhead tried to dart away from the attack but the knife slashed down the side of his top, through the cloth and broke the skin. He let out a cry of sheer terror and pain.

Mozzer jumped back. The attack had taken him by surprise. He hadn't expected the lad to be so up for it but he obviously fancied his chances, even when he was outnumbered. His mate seemed ready to go as well as he fixed a stare on Dean. Mozzer had seen enough. Pinhead was on his toes down the road and Dean's bottle was looking very dodgy.

Wanting out, Dean shouted to Mozzer. 'Mozzer, let's leave it.' Mozzer never liked to do the off but this was a scrap in which he couldn't guarantee a result. He backed off, keeping his eyes firmly fixed on the blade that was now pointing towards him.

'We'll call that a draw, mate, shall we?' It was all he could offer up as a weak attempt to salvage some pride from the situation.

'Call it what you fuckin' like, pal, but remember this face.' With his free hand knife boy pointed towards his own features. 'DON'T EVER FUCK WITH ME AGAIN.' The blade disappeared back into the pocket from where it first came. The two lads then turned away from Mozzer and headed off up towards Oxford Street.

Mozzer turned and shouted after Pinhead. 'COME BACK HERE, YOU LITTLE SHIT.'

11

Mozzer sat staring out of the window of the pub and tried to blank his mind by watching the office girls and shoppers going about their business. Inside he was still shaking. Less than half an hour ago he too had been enjoying himself, out looking for new things to wear. Ten minutes ago he could have found himself lying in a pool of his own blood, and it was all down to Pinhead. Knife boy had shaken him all right, but Pinhead's bottle going angered him even more. One of his troops had done the off and left him and another mate to face the music. Luckily, Dean had just about held it together, otherwise it could have turned into a nightmare.

Dean and Pinhead returned from the toilet where they had been tending his cut arm. Pinhead was in an apologetic mood and clearly had his tail between his legs.

'Mozzer, what can I say? I lost it big time, I know, but that blade took me by . . .'

Mozzer cut him short in a matter-of-fact way. 'Save it, Pinhead, son.'

Pinhead tried to continue. 'Mozzer, let me expl . . .'

Mozzer raised his voice. 'I SAID FUCKIN' SAVE IT, PINHEAD.' All went quiet as Mozzer continued to watch the passing pedestrians. Then he made reference to the wound.

'How bad is it?'

Dean took over. 'It's only a scratch. It'll soon heal up.' There was a silence. 'The top's fucked though.'

'Best you try buying a new one then this time, Pinhead,' replied Mozzer.

'Listen, Mozzer, I am sorry.' Pinhead turned to Dean, then continued. 'I think I better be off and get meself properly sorted out. I'll see you both down the George later, OK?'

'Yeah, OK, Pinhead. See you later.' Dean had played the role of go-between well enough to defuse the situation but knew that Mozzer would provide the best company out of the two for the rest of the afternoon. Mozzer said nothing but continued to make a mental note of just how badly Pinhead had let himself, and his two mates, down. Mozzer's firm had no room for bottlers and so Pinhead was now on his last chance. Pinhead finished his beer then left the pub alone and dejected.

12

The phone rang loudly in Mozzer's ear. Quickly he reached across to kill the noise.

'Ello.' He was still sleepy.

'Mozzer, it's Shep. Sorry to ring so early, mate, but it's Ossie. He's been in hospital all night. They just let him out and we're on our way back home, Mozzer, but it ain't good.'

The bad news shocked Mozzer into life. He sat bolt upright and checked his radio alarm. The LCD display showed 7.36 a.m.

'What's happened and where are you?'

'It's a long story, Mozzer. Julie's here too. She was with him when it happened, so she can fill you in. Mozzer, some cunt's going to pay for this. Can you come round to the house, mate? You won't believe the mess he's in.' Shep's voice was shaking.

'I'm on me way. Try and calm down. I'll get round as quick as I can.'

Mozzer dressed in record time and was soon out the front door.

He walked up the garden path and rang on the bell but as the door was already open he walked straight in.

Shep appeared from the front room. 'Mozzer. I'm sorry it's so early, mate. Thanks for coming.'

'Don't worry. What's the score, then?'

He could hear Julie coming down the stairs, then she joined the two lads. She was a pretty girl, long mousey hair highlighted blonde, about five and a half foot tall. She went straight to Mozzer and put her arms around him. Then the tears started again. The two had known each other for years, long before Ossie had appeared on the scene. Mozzer had often thought of having a pop at her himself over the years but somehow the moment never seemed right and the two had become friends rather than lovers. She was well sorted now with Ossie but Mozzer couldn't help thinking of what might have been. He did his best to reassure her.

'Go on, love, get it all out of your system then you can tell me all about it.' He looked across to Shep. 'Couldn't make a pot of tea, could you?' Shep was also standing in a mixture of deep thought and shock. The request jolted him back to reality.

'Yeah. Yeah, sure, I'll do the honours.' He left the room and Mozzer guided Julie towards the table. After a few moments he started to question her.

'OK, then, are you ready to tell me what happened?'

'Yeah.' She wiped the tears from her eyes then continued. 'We went down the Yo-Yo Club in Streatham last night and . . .'

'Streatham? What the hell were you doing south of the river?'

'We were doing some business, you know, dealing.' She sounded guilty. Julie knew Mozzer didn't mind taking the drugs but also that he thought dealing was a mug's game.

'Fuckin' hell, Julie. Dealing down that neck of the woods for fuck . . .'

This time she cut him short and went on the offensive.

'This place don't pay for itself, you know. We don't all have a cushy little number.'

There was a hint of sarcasm in her voice and the room fell silent. It was a beautiful house and Mozzer knew that the couple must be shifting some serious amounts of gear to pay for its upkeep. Shep had been brought in as a lodger to help pay the bills but his rent would be nowhere near the amount they would have to be pulling in each month.

'I am sorry, Mozzer.' She went on to explain that the two of them had visited the club after being told by a friend that there were plenty of punters to be had, and that the dance floor provided an easy place to work. Usually they wouldn't have gone down with just the two of them but they took the risk and this time it had backfired.

Shep returned with the tea and all three drank as she completed the picture.

After an hour in the club a young girl had approached Ossie and asked him for a couple of pills. He followed her over into the corner to make the deal when suddenly the fire exit door flew open and he was bundled out. The next thing Julie knew, one of the female bouncers came to her and said that her boyfriend would be waiting for her outside. She then grabbed Julie's arm, shoved it up behind her back and marched her out. When she got to the door one of the male bouncers kicked her up the arse and told her never to deal on their patch again. She then looked around for Ossie and found him lying between two parked cars in a pool of blood. She had held it together quite well at first, she said. Calling the police was a definite no-no, so she wrapped his head in her coat and waved down a cab which took them straight to the hospital. Ossie had been carrying 40 pills and had £70 cash on him at the time. The bouncers had taken the lot. All in all, that added up to around £450. Ossie was rushed straight in and had 12 stitches for a wound to the back of his head. The police were called by the hospital but Julie had told them that they had been set upon in the street by a group of lads who had taken a shine to her and a dislike towards her boyfriend. That little tale had kept the hospital staff and (more importantly) the police happy, not that they would have done much to the bouncers if they had known the truth anyway.

Once she had finished Mozzer asked if he could take a look at Ossie. Shep offered to show him up. As they reached the bedroom door, Shep stopped and turned to Mozzer.

'Listen, I am as pissed off about their dealing as anyone. I mean, if the police come through the front door here then I am in the frame as well, OK? But this beating, Mozzer, was well over the top.'

They entered the room to find Ossie fast asleep lying on his right-hand side.

'Bloody hell!' Mozzer could see his face but it looked nothing like the friend he had expected to be going to the football with that afternoon. Both eyes looked like two bruised plums ready to burst open. Across the bridge of his nose were thin white strips holding down a heavy plaster and his lips looked ready to split open if he even tried to speak.

'Is his nose broken?' The two spoke softly so as not to wake the victim.

'Surprisingly not, so they said. But look at this, Mozzer.'

The pair moved around the bed to where they could inspect the head wound. Mozzer could see that the hair had been shaved away so that the surgeon could carry out his duty. He could also see 12 stitches that looked as though they were struggling to hold the flesh together. Blood had worked its way out from the bottom end of the wound and was now staining the pillow.

Mozzer was concerned. 'Is that all right, Shep?'

'They said there may still be a little blood, yeah.' His voice became more concerned. 'That is some whack, Mozzer, don't you think? They reckon he was hit with a piece of piping or a cosh wrapped in rubber. And they don't know what the after-effects could be yet, either.'

'Fuck me, that's nasty. Surely he shouldn't have been allowed home yet.'

'That's what I said, but the hospital said they needed the bed and Julie wanted him home and away from the Old Bill. They have made sure that his own doctor will come around and check on him as well at some time this morning.'

They made their way downstairs to find Julie on the phone to her mum. Mozzer kissed her on the top of the head and told her he would be back early the next morning to check that the pair of them were OK. Then he and Shep went out to his car.

'I can't let that go, Mozzer. He's one of me best mates. As for Chris, Tony and Danny, they don't even know yet. They're going to go off the head, Mozzer. You know what they're like.'

'Course we won't let it go, Shep.' He opened the car door and climbed in. 'I want 15 or 20 of us. I'll pick the right lads at football this afternoon and we'll do the business tonight.' Through the open window he shook Shep's hand. 'Don't worry, mate. It'll be sorted.'

13

DI Young stood with his arms joined around the back as he surveyed the stadium from his vantage point way up in the main stand. This police operations room was state of the art. The hooligans had no place to hide as every angle of the stadium was covered – from here he could even watch the fans taking a piss if he wanted. Inspector Tony Driver was the man in charge.

'Impressive set-up you have here, Tony.'

'Yes. They couldn't pick their noses without us filming it.' The inspector gave the impression of one smug bastard. 'Once this stadium was a war zone. People used to be scared to bring their girlfriends or their children here, but now we have the situation well under control. They wouldn't dare step out of line these days.'

DI Young caught Detective Lopes out of the corner of his eye as a smile crossed his lips. He turned to face the inspector.

'The club still has a poor reputation, does it not, Inspector?'

'A thing of the past. OK, so there are a few hotheads still here but trouble is rare. They know we are watching them while they are in the stadium and so if they want trouble they tend to have it away from here.'

'Do you not monitor them outside, then?' asked Lopes.

The inspector turned to face the young detective whom he had obviously taken an instant dislike to. 'We monitor the crowd as far down the road as the Underground station. Once they are inside the station then they are not ours, but society's problem, Detective.'

DI Young broke the stare that was taking place. 'What about the away supporters? Are you expecting any problems from them today?'

'No. Not many gangs of hooligans come here to cause trouble. We do have their local police with us today as well, but they have informed us that they have no real yobbos here today. We're not expecting any problems whatsoever.'

'Inspector, could you please focus in on one of the areas where the suspected troublemakers sit for me?'

'Certainly.' He moved over to the control panel and ordered one of his staff into action. The image of a group of young men appeared on the bank of television screens. 'We have many potentially violent groups here. They come from various towns, but this lot cause the most problems.' Inspector Driver gave Lopes a sideways glance. 'Mainly at away games might I add.'

DI Young took a closer look, then pointed to the screen. 'Inspector, this is very impressive indeed. Could you enlarge on that group of men there?'

The inspector fell for DI Young's flattery.

'Of course. I could enlarge the image and then make you a print, if you so wish.'

'Really?' The flattery continued. 'No wonder you have the hooligans under control. A print would be most useful, if it's no trouble, that is.'

The inspector was only too pleased that he had impressed his colleague and puffed his chest out.

'I'll assign you this officer. He will print pictures of any face you want. We may even be able to put names to them as well.'

DI Young pointed towards the screen once more.

'Could you put a name to that face?' His finger touched against the image of a face in the centre of the screen.

'Actually I can,' replied the inspector. 'That is a Mr Steven Morris. Otherwise known as Mozzer.'

Lopes joined in. 'Do you have any further information on him?'

The officer at the computer tapped at his keyboard. Data suddenly appeared.

STEVEN MORRIS.

NO PREVIOUS FOOTBALL RELATED ARRESTS BUT THREE PREVIOUS COURT APPEARANCES FOR VIOLENT DISORDER BELIEVED TO BE LINKED TO FOOTBALL.

NO RESTRICTION ORDERS.

NO BANS.

DI Young stood upright then spoke to Detective Lopes.

'Do you recognise that face from Billy Davis's videos?'

'Yes, yes, I do. But judging by the profile he sounds like a bit-player to me.'

'Don't be so sure, Alan. It's the smart ones that never get caught.' He turned his attention back to Inspector Driver. 'Do you know where these lads drink, Inspector?'

'Yes. On match days they drink in various pubs around here, but if you want to catch them all together then your best bet is The George in Ealing. On a Thursday night they tend to meet up and plan their weekends. We have placed the odd spy in there and it's amazing what they come up with.'

The DI looked back at the screen. 'Excellent.' He then turned to Detective Lopes. 'Alan, tell the wife you'll be working late on Thursday.'

14

Mozzer took in the atmosphere of the stadium. It was great to be back and the first Saturday of the season had brought with it all the same old faces. Blackburn had brought a fair few fans but their lads were blending in with the mums and dads as did most mobs when they visited 'The Manor'. Mozzer could never understand firms like that. At home Blackburn were always worth a row but they never came to the capital in numbers and so their reputation would never grow among those that mattered. They saw a trip to the capital as a chance to piss up the weekend and go to some of the top clubs the country had to offer. If they wanted to do some Cockney-bashing then they would do that on their own patch rather than risk the Underground network or the Met police.

Soon the stadium was full and the game under way. City were on the attack from the start and with just two minutes gone forced their first corner. The crowd rose to their feet as the ball flew into the box. The Blackburn keeper punched the ball way outside the box where it was picked up by Travis, the City captain. The midfielder nudged the ball past his marker but before he could dart past he was kicked high into the air.

'YOU DIRTY NORTHERN CUNT.' Clarkie spat the words out. It didn't matter to Clarkie that the offending player was born in France, as far as he was concerned he played for a northern side and therefore he was a northerner. His abuse continued: 'DIRTY NORTHERN FUCKER.'

The girl sitting in front turned around to face him. 'Do you have to shout that in my ear?'

Clarkie stared back in disbelief. 'You what, love?' The girl turned away in disgust. Clarkie turned to Mozzer and laughed. 'Did you hear that? Stupid bitch.'

Her boyfriend turned.

'What did you call her?'

At first Clarkie looked puzzled, then suddenly he took on a new anger.

'I called her a stupid bitch, pal. And I called the northerner a northern cunt. All right?'

The boyfriend suddenly realised that Clarkie was not in

the mood for such a ponce. He had also sussed that he was surrounded by serious back-up. Unfortunately his girlfriend was not so wise.

'Bloody hell, Terry. I am not having some idiot call me that.' She egged her boyfriend on. 'Do something. Go on, do something.'

By now fifteen pairs of eyes were firmly fixed on the slowly shrinking Terry, all awaiting his next move. He turned back to his girlfriend and tried to focus her attention back towards the pitch.

'Leave it, Sandra.'

The girl showed no remorse towards the predicament she had placed him in. 'Oh for Christ's sake. Are you going to let that Neanderthal get away with that?'

He said nothing but the lads of the CBA let forward a chorus of laughter. Once again she turned around, this time shouting directly into Clarkie's face. 'YOU FUCKING PRICK.'

Another chorus of noise came from the lads. 'WOOOOOOOOOO' followed by more laughter. Mozzer had heard enough. He hated these new trendy fans. To him they were taking his game away. Once he used to come to The Manor and enjoy a day standing shoulder to shoulder with the lads on the terraces. Back then he would pay just six quid to get inside and would sing his heart out for the City. Now, thanks to the likes of Terry and his bird, he had to sit on a shite plastic seat and pay over 20 pounds for the privilege. The likes of Terry didn't know the songs or maybe it was just the fact that they were too embarrassed to sing in front of their future wives. Mozzer watched as she continued nagging at her man. He thought these were the kind of people likely to turn up wearing face paint. The type of fans that buy those pathetic clown hats and ask for players' autographs. He also knew that in two to three years' time Terry would have given up on football and would be back shopping or playing golf with the father-in-law on Saturday afternoons rather than supporting City. The passion that football breeds wasn't in Terry's heart. If an opposing fan were to find himself sitting next to Terry then he would probably shake hands and share a drink with him at half-time. Mozzer despised the couple. Back in the good old days if an opposing fan found his way onto the East Bank then the only thing he was likely to be drinking for the next few days would be hospital food through a straw. He leant forward and poured his cup of luke warm tea over their seats. The pair turned around once again, trying to avoid the splash of the liquid.

'Oh for fuck's sake,' Terry shouted.

'Oh dear. Clumsy old me.' Mozzer voiced his concern with total contempt for the pair of them. 'It would seem that in all the excitement I've lost control and spilt my tea all over the place.' His eyes burnt into Terry's face. 'Looks like you'll have to move somewhere else, Terry. Sorry.'

Once again the girl became mouthy. 'YOU FUCKING BASTARDS.' This time there was no laughter from the lads. 'Terry, for fuck . . .' He cut her short and pushed her towards the gangway.

'SHUT THE FUCK UP, SANDRA. JUST MOVE, WILL YOU?'

She looked shocked. 'Don't you dare speak to me like that.' She slapped his face and then, as she turned to leave, took a passing shot at Clarkie. 'YOU WANKER!'

'Now is that any way for a young lady to talk? Honestly, I don't know what the world is coming to.' Clarkie then turned to address the lads. 'I WAS OBVIOUSLY RIGHT. SHE WAS A BITCH.' Once again laughter filled the air.

Mozzer watched as the two made their way up the gangway, arguing as they went. She headed straight towards one of the stewards and Mozzer could see her pointing back towards him. The man in the blue bib took one look and then led the pair away and into a safer part of the stadium. The steward knew that that part of the ground was not a place he would choose to enter. Unlike Terry and Sandra, the steward would be at every game and he knew better than to get on the wrong side of the lads from the CBA.

15

The game had been pretty uneventful. After the long summer wait for the season to start, a 0–0 draw was not exactly what the City fans had hoped for. Outside the stadium things had been quiet. A few northerners had been chased down the side roads by the Under Fives, but as there were no points to be scored in that for the CBA they had left the youngsters to have their fun. Anyway they knew Mozzer had other plans for them. He had assured them that they would have their fix of violence later that night and so now they headed off back to the pub in Ealing for a few jars.

Shep had taken as much information as he could about the Yo-Yo Club from Julie and passed it on to Mozzer. She said there were eight bouncers and just two exits, the front door and the fire escape which led down into the side alley where Ossie had been given his beating. That's all Mozzer needed to know.

'Shep, I want all the lads we're taking in the back room now. You, Danny and the others round them up.'

'Sure thing, Mozzer.' Shep had been on edge all day. The beating his best mate had received had really affected him and he couldn't wait to spill some blood as way of revenge.

Mozzer turned to Baggy. 'Are you sure you want in?'

'Oh yes. I ain't having you lot have all the fun. It'll get me in shape for Leeds next week as well.' Mozzer hadn't expected Baggy to be up for this. If it wasn't to do with football then he usually steered clear. 'Anyway I want to see how Pinhead handles himself after yesterday. If he sits back tonight then he's out on his ear, Mozzer.'

Derek, the pub landlord, often allowed the lads to use the

back room so that they could hold their 'meetings' in private. He was a fair fighter on the terraces himself back in the late '60s, and the CBA gave him the feeling that he was still a bit of a 'Jack The Lad'. He also enjoyed the benefits of having the firm keep his pub trouble-free without having to pay for the honour.

'Rod, watch the door.' As ever Mozzer held court. 'OK, then. We all know what happened to Ossie. Believe me, he took a right hiding last night. If you saw the state of him you would know that these bouncers are no mugs. We all have to be on the case so don't get too shit-faced. Anyone that's pissed ain't coming, right?' He scouted the room as all 15 lads nodded back in approval. A feeling of warmth came over him as that buzz rose for the first time in his stomach. These were *his* lads and they listened to his every word.

'What's the story at the club then, Mozzer?' Stokey was the lad in the firm who had the most bottle. He always wanted to know the layout of any pub or club that the firm hit. Without exception he would be the first one to offer himself up when a place needed scouting and that often resulted in him taking the odd hiding if the opposition sussed him out. Amazingly, more often than not he came out smelling of roses and within the firm he was a bit of a hero. Mozzer thought that Stokey got off on the danger more than anyone else he had ever known and was surprised that the lad had only once ended up serving time at one of Her Majesty's 'hotels'.

'Apparently there are eight bouncers – seven blokes and one tart. As far as getting in is concerned, there are only two doors – the front entrance and the fire exit at the back. The fire exit is where they take punters out and give them a hiding, as it leads out into a back alley which is well hidden from the main drag. That's all Julie could tell us.' Mozzer offered up a question. 'Has anyone else ever been down this place?'

Kelly piped up. 'Yeah. I've been down there a fair few times, Mozzer, with the bird. One of the bouncers is a total nutter. I've seen him in action loads of times. I tell ya, lads, he loves it. And he is fuckin' massive.'

'So fucking what. The bigger they are the harder they fall, Kelly.' Danny sounded angry as he bit at his mate. 'The cunt won't be so mouthy when he gets this around his head.' In his hand he held a leather-bound cosh. As he slapped the end into the palm of his hand the thud brought no emotion to his face. Wrapped up in the leather was a lead ball about one and a half inches in diameter and Danny was obviously in the mood to use it. Baggy looked at Mozzer. Danny never usually needed the aid of a weapon but the attack on one of his best mates had fired an anger that Baggy had never seen before.

Kelly continued. 'Easy, Danny, I am only telling you, mate. He's a white guy, six foot ten, about 18 stone and built like a brick shithouse. Danny, he's yours if you want him.'

Chris joined in. 'He's ours, Kelly.' He put his arm around Danny to give added support.

'What about the rest of them, Kelly? Do you reckon they'll be tooled-up?' Baggy asked, wanting to ease the tension.

'Oh yeah, I am sure of that, Baggy.'

Mozzer started to put his plan to the rest of the firm. 'Right. I'll take four in my motor, the rest of you go down in the back of Baggy's van. We do the off from here at 10.30. This is what we do . . .'

16

As the lads made their way up the High Road they split into smaller groups. Mozzer took up position in a shop doorway opposite the entrance as Stokey and Dean entered the club. With him he had Baggy, Pinhead and Camden. All four stood in silence as they fixed their eyes on the front door. Inside their bodies the buzz was rising. Danny, Chris and Shep arrived just as the large bouncer appeared from the door.

'Fuck me. He is a big 'un.' Baggy was almost laughing as the adrenalin took hold.

'If that's him, Baggy,' replied Mozzer, then he turned to Camden. 'You take him, OK?' The young lad didn't know whether his mentor was serious or not. He hoped not and let out a nervous laugh. Once again they fell silent. The bouncer started to give Chris the large one.

Baggy spoke under his breath. 'Fuck. I hope Danny holds it together.'

Danny wanted the row there and then but he knew he had a bigger job to do. He fought hard to contain the desire to crack the skull of this meat-head standing before him. The cosh had been placed so that the ball was resting firmly between his arse cheeks. If the bouncer bent down and reached around there then Danny would bring up his knee and spread his nose across the pavement. Finally he was given the all-clear and made his way up the stairs to the pay desk. Chris and Shep followed. Mozzer's mobile rang. It was Stokey.

'Sussed it, Mozzer. There ain't that many people in here yet so it should be easy. It's a shame we have to total the place though, as there's a fair bit of crumpet in here. Could we hold on for a few hours, Mozzer, so I can try my luck?'

Mozzer could never get to grips as to how Stokey remained so calm just before a row and his own nervousness brought a stern reply.

'Shut the fuck up, you nonce. Listen, Danny and the lads have just got in. Give it five minutes then kick it off.'

'Just an hour then, Mozzer, go on.' He started laughing. Then the phone went dead. Stokey looked at Dean and tutted. 'Fucking spoil-sport.'

Mozzer looked back down the road to see Kelly, Charlie and Greg standing in one doorway, while Tony, Rod and Clive waited outside the off-licence. All eyes were fixed on the bouncers at the front door.

Inside, Dean made eye contact with Danny then pointed

towards the bouncer they had decided to target. The three lads bought lager but were sad to see the liquid delivered in plastic glasses. Chris checked the bucket full of empty bottles.

'Could be worth remembering, lads.' All three turned to watch Stokey and Dean move among the punters jumping around on the dance floor. Dean moved towards his target. The easy option would be to lay one on the bouncer there and then, but Mozzer had laid down the law. The plan was to lure all the bouncers away from the front door and out the back of the club. The other three lads at the bar moved towards the fire exit. Dean's shoulder smacked hard against the bouncer's back. Sharply he turned, grabbing Dean by the jacket.

'WATCH YOUR FUCKIN' STEP, YOU PRAT.' He spat the words into Dean's face, then pushed him away.

'FUCK YOU,' came Dean's reply. 'FUCKING HARD MAN, ARE YA? HARD MAN WITH ALL YOUR FUCKIN' BACK-UP.' His arms stretched wide as he egged the bouncer on. 'WOULDN'T BE SO FUCKING MOUTHY ONE ON ONE OUT THE FUCKIN' BACK, WOULD YOU?'

The bouncer was at first surprised by the smaller lad's reaction, then the thought of dishing out a battering so early on in the evening suddenly started to appeal to him. He looked around to summon up his troops. Already they were moving forward. Outside the giant turned and shot through the door and up the stairs followed by a smaller lad and the lady bouncer. That was the signal Mozzer had been waiting for. It was time to make their move. He shot a look down the road as he crossed to see the other six lads head down the alley to the back of the club. Baggy pulled a balaclava over his head and followed behind. He was well up for the row, but he wasn't going to risk his business getting a revenge pay-back visit. Inside Stokey had joined in the pushing and shoving as the bouncers grabbed at them. The clubbers moved quickly out the way. Girls started screaming, crying and shouting.

Suddenly he could see more of the club's bouncers heading towards them, and at the front was the giant. Dean was going well but Stokey pulled him back towards the fire exit.

'GET THE FUCK OUT, YOU PRAT.' Both the lads turned and shot towards the fire escape but two of the bouncers made it there before them and kicked the doors open. Danny could see the giant bearing down on his two friends. In his hand he held a piece of pipe about 18 inches long. The sight triggered Danny's mind.

'It was you, you bastard,' he said to himself. He could hold back no longer. The leather strap on the cosh was firmly wrapped around his wrist and he gripped the handle tight. He timed his strike to perfection. As the bouncer approached at speed, Danny swung the cosh. The lead ball smashed directly into the mouth. The cracking of teeth sent a shock wave down Danny's fingers. A shot of joy and hatred pumped in his stomach at the same time. The giant dropped the pipe and staggered backwards. Shep jumped him, grabbing his neck and dragging him to the floor.

'HIT THE FUCKER AGAIN, FOR FUCK'S SAKE. HE AIN'T OUT YET.'

He sounded desperate but Danny didn't need telling twice. He pounced on his prey. *Crack.* The lead hit the temple. *Crack.* It hit home again. Then again, again. Shep let go and rose to his feet then pulled Danny off. The giant lay totally still.

'Enough, Danny. It's going off out the back. COME ON.'

Danny stared down. He couldn't recognise the face as that of the big man who had been so mouthy to him at the door. All he could see lit by the lights of the disco was a pool of blood, ripped flesh and broken teeth.

'CUNT.' He launched one last kick into what was once the face of the body on the floor. He knew that he was the man who had made his best mate suffer last night and that last kick was Ossie's.

Mozzer steamed through the front door and up the stairs.

The girl taking the money shot back, scared, as Baggy and Camden charged up behind him. Pinhead rammed the doors shut and searched out the lock. Then he bolted the doors and stood watch. The bouncers had left the girl unprotected. As she reached for the phone Mozzer grabbed her hands. He shouted at her.

'LEAVE THE FUCKIN' PHONE ALONE AND SHUT THE FUCK UP.' The girl cowered down onto the floor and started to cry. 'Now if you're a good girl you won't get hurt.'

Camden had opened the club doors in order to see the chaos inside. Mozzer pushed him forward.

'Go on, son, get in there.'

Camden was off like a rocket.

'Baggy, you take care of her. And get the fucking money while you're at it.'

Baggy jumped the counter and once again the girl flinched. He too shouted at the girl. 'HAVE YOU GOT CAMERAS ON THE DOOR HERE? IF SO, WHERE'S THE FUCKIN' VIDEO?' She pointed to a cupboard above where she was squatting. Baggy opened the door. Next to the video was a television screen and the picture relayed the battle taking place at the back of the club. He looked down at the girl, his voice now calm. 'We'll leave that running a while I think, love.' He then turned and opened the till before stuffing the notes into his pockets. Pinhead joined him and started looking in all the other drawers for anything else of value. Suddenly, there before him was a bag full of pills.

'I think I know who these may belong to, don't you?' He held the bag up for Baggy to see.

'I ain't touching them, you can carry 'em.'

Pinhead stuffed the pills into his jacket. 'Do you need me here, Baggy?'

Baggy looked back and smiled. He was pleased to know that Pinhead had got his bottle back.

'No. You go enjoy yourself.'

With that the lad shot through the door and into the

darkness. Baggy turned and ripped the phone from the wall.

Kelly and the rest of the lads arrived at the bottom of the fire escape just as the doors flew open. He stopped the lads sharp.

'Hang on. Let's get them all in view first.' He peered around the corner to see the girl bouncer and the younger lad run out and onto the stairs. Stokey and Dean were the next to appear, followed by four more of the club staff. The boots and fists were flying. The bouncers clearly thought this was going to be their night, for them a spot of easy early evening entertainment. After all they had the greater numbers and six against two were fairly safe odds. They pushed and pulled at Stokey and Dean to get them to the bottom of the staircase. As they arrived, Kelly and the lads sprung their trap. The bouncers didn't know what hit them. Two of them panicked and tried to make a run for it but had no chance. Kelly and the lads had come well tooled-up. Greg swung the bike chain above his head then down across the face of his target. The bouncer's head jerked back and he let out a horrific scream as the metal tore at his flesh. His hands came up trying to pull the metal away but Greg yanked the chain back and the lad's head followed, hitting the wall. Rod continued the attack, letting his boots fly repeatedly. Thankfully for the bouncer, the collision with the brick had blanked him out. He wouldn't be feeling the thudding blows now – that pain would have to wait for the morning.

Clive and Charlie were working hard to add to the casualties as Camden appeared at the top of the stairs. He had seen many great battles in his time with the Juniors but nothing like this. This was where he wanted to be, fighting it out with the big boys, and if he wanted to stay then he would have to prove himself. Mozzer arrived to see the young lad steam down the stairs and jump on the back of the last standing bouncer, who was still slugging away with Stokey. This was what Mozzer lived for. Like a general, he surveyed the situation. Pinhead shot past him, nearly knocking him over in his eagerness to make his mark. He watched for about half a minute. Below all he could see were his troops landing kick after kick into the bodies of the bouncers, now either motionless or curled up in tight balls so as to soften the relentless attack. Even the female bouncer suffered. He knew that his lads took no prisoners. They knew that a female bouncer could inflict as much damage as anyone else. She chose her occupation and she certainly wouldn't have shed any tears for Ossie last night.

Mozzer turned and headed back through the club to the pay desk. 'BAGGY, LET'S GO.'

'Hang on. I'll just get this.' He leant forward, switched off the video and took the cassette from the machine. 'You're gonna love this.'

The girl was still curled up in the corner, shaking. Mozzer crouched down to give her his final message.

'Now listen, love, and listen good. You won't ever be seeing us again or getting another visit from us, OK? You tell your people we ain't interested in this manor. We ain't interested in the club and we ain't drug dealers. We paid you a visit because you picked the wrong person to fuck with last night. Simple as that, understand?' Mozzer nodded at the girl. She nodded back. 'Now one last thing. If one of my lads gets even so much as a scratch for what happened tonight then I am telling you this club is history. Tell them I've got plenty more lads than this if they want to make a war of it. As far as I am concerned that's end of story.'

He rose to his feet. Throughout the message he had sounded calm but now more urgency filled his voice. 'BAGGY LET'S GO.' The two lads ran back through the club and down the fire exit. Most of the other lads were now waiting out in the main drag, leaving just Pinhead and Danny to keep watch over the pile of bodies.

Once out in the street the group spread out and moved

quickly back to their transport. The hit had taken less than ten minutes but it had seemed like ages. The stories would last much longer. Mozzer's planning had assured that the firm had come away mostly unscathed, only Stokey had suffered any real blows. Mozzer knew he needed cleaning up and so they would drive him back west to the pub in Ealing. Stokey piled into the back of Mozzer's motor along with Pinhead and Dean. Charlie took the front seat. The engine fired up and the car sped off back north of the river followed by the Transit. Inside the vehicle the noise was deafening as each lad tried to tell the rest about the part he had played in the victory.

'Lads, you were *all* the bollocks. I am proud of every one of ya.'

As the car crossed Battersea Bridge the lads let go with the customary cheer. The injuries to his eye and lip had not curbed Stokey's excitement. 'WAY HAY . . . Smell that clean air. I feel better already, lads.'

Mozzer then burst into song and the rest joined the chorus.

. . . I SAID WE ARE THE C-B-A. THE FAMOUS C-B-A . . .

17

When the lads arrived back they found the regulars at The George enjoying the usual late night lock-in.

'Line them up, Derek, will ya?' Mozzer placed an order before moving off to the back room with his right-hand man. Baggy emptied his pockets out on the table then the two counted the cash.

'Fuck me, Mozzer. There must be over three grand here.'

'Result. This must be last night's takings as well.' The two laughed with excitement. 'What do you say we give the lads a hundred quid each then use the rest for travelling next week?'

Baggy agreed and so the two started to split the money into equal piles, setting an extra amount aside to pay for the bar order Mozzer had just placed.

'Oh, I almost forgot.' Baggy reached inside his jacket and pulled out the video cassette. 'Give this to Ossie when you see him. It should cheer him up a bit.'

Mozzer sounded excited at the thought of seeing his lads in action again. 'Oh fuck, yeah. I'll get some copies run out as well. Nice one.' He had one last question for Baggy. 'How did Pinhead do out front?'

Baggy looked up and smiled. 'No worries, Mozzer, he was chumping to get in there and do his bit.'

'Good.' He counted out an extra pile of cash. 'Send him in for a word, will ya?'

Baggy left the room, leaving Mozzer with nothing but his thoughts. Soon Pinhead poked his head around the door and broke the silence. He sounded nervous, as if he were expecting a bollocking.

'What's up, Mozzer?'

'Nothing. I just want a word, that's all. Come in and shut the door.' The lad walked forward. 'Listen. You did well tonight. Me and Baggy are proud of ya, Pinhead.' He could see the relief flow through his body. Mozzer then held out his hand. Clutched in his fist was a bundle of notes. 'That Duffer jacket. Go treat yourself on Monday.' He gave the money to Pinhead.

'Fucking hell, Mozzer.' The lad couldn't believe his luck. 'Are you sure?'

'You earned it, son. Take the money.'

Pinhead suddenly remembered the bag of pills he had taken from the club. He explained that he thought they must be the pills taken from Ossie the night before. Mozzer took one of the pills from the bag and gave it a closer inspection.

'Fuck me. These are Bulldogs. I ain't had these for ages.' He looked up at Pinhead. 'Fancy going clubbing?'

18

Mozzer loved this club. The End always provided him with the best Drum and Bass London had to offer. The security were attitude-free and the vibe of the punters was sweet. More importantly, the music always hit the spot. Pinhead and the others headed off to the bar as Mozzer surveyed the club. He never mixed drink and pills. He liked to keep his system clean in order to give the Ecstasy a free run through his body. They had popped a pill just after parking up and the music was starting to give the drug its first lift. Tony returned with a bottle of water from which Mozzer took a few short sips. He moved down onto the dance floor in order to check out the visuals showing above the mixing desk. He took more sips from the plastic bottle, then clocked the punters dancing around him. The lads in front, the girl at his side. He shot a glance over his shoulder. The lad behind smiled and Mozzer returned the gesture. More water. The sub bass was working on his mind. All thoughts of the violence he had witnessed that day were banished. He closed his eyes and felt a smile cross his lips. His body began to sway from side to side to the tunes being spun by the DJ Hype. The white pills with the brown speckle were just as Mozzer remembered. If only all pills were like this.

Dean joined him and shouted at the top of his voice as if to announce his arrival to the rest of the punters already buzzing to the music. 'OI, OI.' He then turned to Mozzer. 'Is this the fuckin' bollocks or what, eh, Mozzer?'

Mozzer said nothing. He just smiled at his friend then turned to focus back on the visuals. The rush was welling up in his veins. His body took on a mind of its own as it began to gel with the beats pumping through his head. More water. He closed his eyes once more as his mind talked back to him about his happiest thoughts. His body suddenly jolted as a shock shot down his spine. He thought of those dancing around him sharing his experience. He was one of them. He wanted to be one of them. The rush was getting stronger. He took short sharp breaths. More water. Again he checked those dancing around him. More smiles. More breath. The End was banging, the music full on. The rush welling up, getting stronger. He stood straighter. The surge shook through him. His body jumped to the music. Had he ever felt so happy? So content? Nothing else on the earth mattered. Nothing entered his mind but the beat of the music. The feeling of being part of this joyous mass of dancing bodies surrounded him. His heart banged away inside. The blood rushed through him.

The DJs were relentless, lifting the crowd then dropping them down, only offering enough time to compose themselves before bringing on the next rush. Time was lost on Mozzer. He danced. He drank more water. He smiled and shook the hands of those around him. Mozzer lost himself within parts of his mind that never usually spoke to him. The feeling was beautiful. Could he really be this man so in love with violence? Joy washed over him time after time, then suddenly the lights of the club came on and the music stopped. Pinhead, Tony and Dean were still with him. So now there was a calmer, warmer feeling. It was 5.15 a.m. and the August day was just breaking through. Mozzer took deep breaths and puffed his chest out as the group talked and walked the streets towards the all-night supermarket opposite Holborn tube. The afterglow of the pill, the club and the dancing washed over Mozzer. A beautiful feeling. Dean soaked up the warmth of the early morning as he strutted forward, his shirt tied around his waist. The lads bought biscuits and fruit juice before jumping back into Mozzer's car and heading back home.

He dropped the rest of the lads at Dean's flat then made his way back to his place in Greenford. He took a shower, switched on the television and drank tea. His head started to rock forward as the first waves of tiredness crept over him. He shook his head, got to his feet and made his way to the bedroom. One look at the double bed confirmed his desire to crash out. He climbed beneath the duvet, felt the warmth surround him and closed his eyes. The day had passed.

19

Mozzer checked his watch as he pulled up outside Ossie's house. It was 1.48 p.m. He was surprised to see Shep's blue Escort parked down the road. He rang the bell and Shep answered the door, looking a little the worse for wear.

'Bloody hell, Shep. I am glad I didn't wake up with you on me face this morning.' He had expected Shep and the lads to be enjoying the usual Sunday afternoon session down at The George.

'Ah don't. It was a late one. God knows when we left. I feel like shit and I ain't ever drinking again.'

Mozzer laughed. How many times had he said or heard that comment? He walked into the kitchen to find Danny and Chris looking equally horrible. Standing by the kettle making tea was Ossie.

'Mozzer, how's it going?' He was delighted to see the main man. 'Look at these wankers. They look worse than I do.' The truth was that they didn't. Ossie looked a mess. The bruising and the swelling was at its peak.

'How you feeling?'

'Actually not too bad. My head aches most of all. The doctor said it should be OK, but he's booked me in down the hospital to have a scan later on.'

Danny politely tried to make conversation. 'Where did you end up, Mozzer?'

'Down The End. Blinding night.'

Danny wasn't really interested but offered some kind of reply. 'Oh. Nice one.' Then he returned his stare at the table. Mozzer laughed as he pulled the video from his pocket.

'Fuck me, the state of you three. To think you were in such good fighting form last night. I reckon my two three-year-old nephews could beat the shit out of you lot this morning.'

Ossie clocked the video in his visitor's hand.

'What's that, Mozzer?'

'Well, Ossie, I suppose you must have heard the story of last night, yeah? Well, now see the video.'

Danny looked up. 'You what?'

'Baggy pinched this video from the club. It's got all last night's action on it.' He waved the cassette in the air for all to see.

Chris spoke for the first time as the three pissheads suddenly came to life. 'You are joking?' He turned to Ossie. 'Ossie, please say your video's working, please.' He sounded excited and desperate.

'Fuckin' right, it is. Let's have a look.' Suddenly the kitchen sprung into life as they all made a dash for the living-room.

The battle at the Yo-Yo Club was better than even Mozzer had remembered. He had surrounded himself with violent people and they clearly loved to see themselves in action. Danny was pissed off because his attack had taken place inside the club. Ossie confirmed via the description given that he had indeed sorted the right man and couldn't contain his pleasure at seeing the bastards who had beaten him getting hammered. As the lads watched the video over and over, Mozzer signalled to Ossie that he wanted a word in private and they made their way to the kitchen. As Ossie put the kettle on, Mozzer started the conversation.

'Where's Julie?'

'She's down her mum's for dinner. I was meant to go but she told her I had the trots.'

'Right.' He paused for a moment to collect his composure, then continued the conversation. 'Ossie, I have to say this, mate. Don't you think you were some kind of cunt going down there with no back-up?'

'Mozzer, I was told it was safe.'

'Well, whoever told you needs a word, son. Look at the state of ya. Stokey ain't looking too good, either.' The room fell silent for a few seconds. Mozzer then pulled the bag of pills from his pocket and held them up for Ossie to see. 'Pinhead thinks these are yours.' Ossie showed no remorse for the beating Stokey had received, only joy at the return of his pills.

'Ah, nice one.' He reached for the bag but Mozzer pulled it away.

'I don't think you realise what I just said. We put ourselves up for you last night because you acted like a cunt on Friday. Stokey probably won't get a shag for the next six months because his face is a mess and all you seem to care about are your fuckin' pills.' He threw the bag on the table and the room fell silent once more.

'Mozzer, I am sorry. I ain't quite with it yet. I'll ring Stokey, Pinhead and all the lads later. Honest.'

Mozzer didn't want to argue. Ossie was the salt of the earth but the attitude he had adopted was not what Mozzer had expected.

'And what about Julie? How would you feel if she had taken a hiding, eh?'

Ossie suddenly went on the defensive. He had seen the way the two looked at each other from time to time and he knew that Julie had had a thing about Mozzer in the past.

'She knows the rules. It's how we earn our money, Mozzer. It pays for this place, her clothes, her car, everything. Sometimes it goes tits up.'

Mozzer shook his head and sighed. 'You're a fucking idiot.' There was no point in continuing. 'Ah well, I ain't come here to argue with you. I better be off.' He held out his hand and the two shook. 'Just be more careful, Ossie.' Peace had been made.

'Yeah, noted. I'll make those calls today. And Mozzer, cheers. I owe you one.'

'No you don't.' He poked his head around the living-room

door and said goodbye to the rest of the lads then headed off down the hallway. Before Mozzer left the house he shouted back one last message to Ossie. 'Oh by the way, me, Pinhead, Dean and Tony took two pills each.'

'Cheeky bastards. That's 80 quid you owe me.'

'Bollocks, it is.'

20

Billy watched through his ground-floor window as DI Young, Detective Lopes and one other policeman walked towards his front door. The visit from the police had put him on edge. On this occasion he hadn't had time to relocate his crop of plants and so they remained hidden within the purpose-built growing units that stood in the spare bedroom. His main worry was the sweet unmistakable odour given off by his wage-earner. The door to the room was locked and the extractor fan was humming away for all it was worth, so all Billy could do was hope. The doorbell rang and Billy ushered the officers in. DI Young was acting in his usual pleasant way.

'Mr Davis, this officer is Detective Hunt. He will be placing the trace on your telephone.' The two men exchanged nods. 'You are expecting the call at midday, yes?'

'Yeah. He won't be late.'

'Who won't?' Lopes tried to catch Billy off guard but the Londoner didn't answer.

DI Young continued.

'What information have you gathered for him, Billy?'

'The Leeds firm are going after Stoke this Saturday.'

Lopes fired the next question. 'And how did you find that out, Billy?'

'There was more talk about that down the local this weekend than anything else. Leeds, Stoke. That's a big one. London wanted to know if the Leeds lads were travelling by train through Crewe. That I don't know.'

DI Young thought for a while. 'Right, tell him they are.' He turned to Lopes. 'That way we can get a good view of the gang at least.'

Lopes turned once more on Billy. 'Is that it?'

'Yes.' Billy then started to explain himself. 'Look, this stuff is easy to find out. You lot should know the score.' The officers remained silent and just stared back at him. The thought of the weed being discovered weighed heavily on Billy's mind as he tried to appease the two men. 'I tell you this, the Stoke firm know what's going down as well. They will be out in numbers and if it goes off then it will be the row to end all rows.'

DI Young suddenly turned the conversation to another topic. 'Before we start, Billy, I have some photographs I would like you to look at.' He opened his briefcase, pulled out a yellow folder and set it down on the table. The three men sat themselves down as Hunt went to work on the telephone. DI Young laid out 20 photographs on the table.

'I want to go through these one by one, Billy. Tell me if you recognise any of these faces.'

Billy checked the images. He saw Clarkie, Tony, Baggy. Of the 20 photographs he must have known at least 15 of the faces but one stood out more than any other, and that was the picture of Mozzer.

'Well, Billy?' DI Young tried to gain some reaction from his host.

'Come on, Billy boy. DI Young wants an answer.' Lopes continued with his threatening attitude. Billy had no choice but to play the game.

'Yes, I do. Of course I do, some of these lads are the lads in the videos I've had.'

'Well, then, point out the faces you know so that DI Young can ask their names.'

'I've told you I don't know any names. I can help you with faces but not names.'

Lopes became agitated. 'Billy, we all know that's bullshit. Now give us a few names.'

Billy looked at the DI. 'Look, the only thing I could do is recognise the voice of London. To do that I'd have to be talking to him face to face, wouldn't I?' Billy had pushed his luck too far as Lopes called his bluff.

'Well, that is not such a bad idea actually, Billy.' He sat back in his seat as DI Young watched the battle of wits unfold before him. 'Let's say I give you the benefit of the doubt. Say you don't know them and more importantly for you, Billy, they don't know you. Therefore you wouldn't mind coming down to London with me and sitting among these "faces", would you? That way we may be able to put a face to the voice.'

Billy had dug himself into a bad situation. If he so much as stepped one foot inside The Manor he would find himself surrounded by old friends and faces eager to catch up on old times. Many of those friends were staring back at him now through the photographs on the table.

'Sure. If that's what you want.' The deep swallow Billy had taken was not lost on DI Young. He joined the conversation.

'I have a better idea, Billy. Do you know The George pub in Ealing?' Billy's stomach tightened. He acted as a man struggling to find the space in his brain where the information might be kept, pursed his lips and shook his shoulders. Of course he knew The George but his answer denied it.

'No. I don't think I do.'

'You don't think so.' Lopes paused. Billy knew the two men had seen through him. 'Well, in that case it might be better if we take you there then, Billy. It won't be so hit and miss if you know what I mean?'

Billy played ignorant. 'Sure. If it will help, I'll do it.'

Detective Hunt broke the tense atmosphere. 'We're all set here now.'

Billy could see Lopes' eyes burning into him as DI Young

answered. 'Excellent.' He checked his watch. 'Ten minutes to 12.'

Lopes got to his feet. 'Can I use your toilet, please, Mr Davis?'

'Yes, sure.' Billy was fazed by the conversation that had just taken place. He shook himself back and into control. 'I'll show you.' Billy pointed the door out and watched as Lopes made his way down the hall and past the spare bedroom. He stayed by the door so that he could keep an eye on the hallway and the two officers in the lounge. Billy heard the chain flush then saw Lopes reappear. On his way back down the passageway Lopes suddenly stopped by the spare room and took a long slow breath. A wry grin came on his face.

'Um. Such a sweet smell, Billy.' The odour was unmistakable. Billy's heart jumped, then Lopes continued his walk forward. As he passed he offered some advice. 'You must open more windows, Billy. You never know who might come through the door when you least expect it.' Now Billy badly wanted the coppers out of his flat, as the morning could hardly have gone any worse for him.

The phone rang. All three men stared at Billy. Detective Hunt was the only one to speak.

'Try to keep him talking for as long as possible.' Hunt had rigged the phone so that everyone could hear the conversation.

Billy picked up the receiver. 'Hello.'

'Hello. London here.' It was Mozzer's voice. 'Have you got any info for me?' All eyes were fixed on Billy.

'Yes. Leeds are at Stoke next week.'

'Excellent. Anything else you can tell me?' Billy looked at the officers. DI Young nodded back.

'Yes, Crewe would be a good place to visit.'

'Lovely.' Billy was desperately trying to think of a way to let Mozzer know that the conversation was being relayed directly into the ears of the filth, but there was no way out.

Detective Hunt sat back and shook his head in disappointment.

'Is that all you have?' Mozzer continued.

'No. Stoke are playing as well that day.'

'Really?' Mozzer had sounded surprised at first, then excited. 'Excellent. Anything else?'

'No, that's all I have.'

'Right. Cheers then. I'll be in touch.'

'Yeah, cheers.' Suddenly the phone went dead. Billy replaced his handset as Young and Lopes looked towards Detective Hunt. DI Young spoke first.

'What's wrong?'

'It's a mobile. Can't trace it.'

Lopes let his disappointment show as he slapped the side of the chair. 'Bollocks.' He turned on Billy. 'You could have kept him talking longer, Davis.'

Detective Hunt calmed the officer down.

'It wouldn't have mattered. I would never have got it. Sorry, but there's just nothing you can do with some of these new mobiles phones.'

21

Mozzer placed the mobile back into the case hanging from his belt, then re-ran the conversation over in his head.

> *. . . Yes . . . Game on . . . Stoke will be at it as well, sweet . . . Baggy's gonna love this . . . We'll need big numbers. Big numbers . . . I'll give the other firms the nod, we'll need 'em . . . Crewe Station, game on . . . fucking game on . . .*

He suspected nothing. He took a long breath of fresh air then climbed back into his car. He loved being on the road on days like this. It hadn't taken Mozzer long to get to the position he now held within the company. Being area sales manager was an easy ride for a man of his confidence and ability. He still liked to keep the odd client from the old days, just to keep his hand in. But now his main purpose was to check on the other sales representatives, give them training and make sure they were not taking the piss with time off. For a man with such a passion for football the job was ideal as it allowed Mozzer time to organise plans for the CBA's next 'fixture'. He checked himself in the mirror. He was looking good. His hair was cropped close at a clipper number two length, and his skin was as smooth as a baby's arse. Mozzer had always liked a beer, but he kept himself in shape and although he was now 29 his fitness routine gave him the appearance of a man two or three years younger. Today he wore his favourite sky blue Ben Sherman shirt. He loved the cut, it looked class and the button-down collar meant that he didn't need the stuffiness of a tie. Mozzer hated wearing ties, it reminded him of his school days and authority. He enjoyed his time at school and had worked hard but the uniform, the tie, the pettiness of stupid rules had turned him away at the last moment. Mozzer was never one to conform. In his final year the teachers had started to make it hard for the lad who would never let anything go unchallenged and so he gave up on examinations and trusted only himself. He often wished that he could go back and grab those same teachers by the neck and show them how far he had managed to get, despite their efforts to break him. Deep down he also acknowledged that it was their constant disbelief in his ability that drove him to get to where he was now.

Mozzer dialled the number and got the girl on reception.

'Hello, Avionics, can I help you?'

'Yes. Could I speak to Peter Stanard, warehouse manager, please?'

'Please hold.' Mozzer heard the girl announce the call over the company public address system, her voice echoing through the building, then music began to play in Mozzer's ear. Thirty seconds later the call was answered.

'Hello.' Despite living in a Hertfordshire new town Peter Stanard had a voice that was as Cockney as Mike Reid.

'Peter, Mozzer here. CBA.'

'Hello, Mozzer.' His voice came alive. 'What can I do for ya, pal?'

'We've got something on this Saturday, it's a big 'un and we need numbers. I wondered if your lot were up for it?'

'Sounds sweet. Who, where and what?'

'Listen, have you had lunch yet? If not I'll take you for a pint as I'd rather talk about this face to face.'

'Fair enough. I can take lunch at either one or two. You know where I am, don't ya?'

'Yeah. I'll be up at one, then.' Mozzer switched off the mobile and then started the engine.

22

The officers slowly got their belongings together and made their way out of the flat.

'Billy, we will be in touch. If you have any more information then give us a call, OK?' DI Young's words sounded to Billy like those of his old schoolmaster.

'Sure thing.'

'Be seeing you, Billy.' Lopes couldn't resist one last dig. 'And don't forget to have your bag ready for a trip back home.'

Billy's stomach turned. The hate he felt for Lopes was getting stronger by the second. Billy closed the door and breathed a huge sigh of relief. He gathered himself, then went to check his plants. As he got to the door he sniffed the air. The sweet smell filled his lungs as it had Detective Lopes'. He opened the door and there they were, all his babies safe and sound. How could he have been so stupid? He shook his head then closed the door. What Lopes had said about being paid another visit had burned into Billy's mind. He would need to start making plans sooner than he had hoped.

Lopes was the first to speak as the car pulled away. 'Well, if you ask me I think Davis knows every one of those lads in the pictures.'

'I think you're right, Alan. That was an excellent stunt threatening him with a trip down south.'

The young detective felt proud of himself.

'Well, what do you think? Should we take him down to The George pub this week?'

'No, definitely not. If we're right, and I believe we are, then everyone in the pub will know him and our operation will be blown. It's too much of a risk at this stage.'

Lopes immediately felt put back in his place and so tried to score more brownie points.

'Did you notice the smell in the flat, Detective Inspector?'

'We're not interested in drugs. The Drug Squad had their shot at Billy Davis. Now we have him and I am not jeopardising that for a cheap drugs conviction.'

23

Thursday night and once again the pub was crammed. The main topic of conversation was the hit on the night club the previous weekend, as those involved bathed in the glory of what had now become a famous night in the history of the firm. There were a few lads playing up and pissed off at the fact they had not been asked to take part, but none dared mention that to Mozzer's face. Ossie had ventured out for the first time since his beating. His face was still a mess but inside he felt fine as he paid his gratitude back by buying pints of lager for those who had gone into battle for him. Mozzer had spoken to Baggy at length on the phone about the conversation with his contact and now the two were finalising their plans.

'I've contacted the main men from all the other firms and

they are well up for it. My only main worry is that we'll have loads of hangers-on and glory hunters. I've been to see Hemel Peter and he was well up for it. I trust him to bring only his top 20 lads but if the other firms bring too many then the police will be all over us.'

'Don't worry, it won't happen. The other firms have a reputation to maintain, Mozzer. We wouldn't turn up with a load of Muppets would we?' Mozzer shook his head in agreement. 'Well, then, nor would they. It's Leeds and Stoke we need to worry about. Who are we taking?'

'Everyone we can trust. If you see anyone hanging on who you don't fancy then fuck 'em off. I'll do the same. OK? We have to get a result Saturday.' His voice spoke with determination and passion. 'I'll get the beers in.' He left Baggy at the table and made for the bar.

Derek quickly came to his service. 'Mozzer, how's things?'

'Sweet Derek, sweet. Two of the usual.'

The landlord took two clean glasses from the shelf and started to pull the drinks from the tap.

'Mozzer, don't look now but have you clocked the two blokes over in the corner by the window?'

Mozzer didn't turn but inside he was burning with curiosity.

'No. Why?'

'Well, I hadn't seen them before today but they were in here at dinner time as well. They ain't drinking proper, Mozzer.' He paused for a while as he masterfully pulled the pint from its tap. 'Now I've been in this game for over 20 years and two visits in one day without buying anything stronger than a shandy says one thing to me: Old Bill.'

Mozzer was desperate to look round but managed to resist. He leant on the bar and bounced on his toes to curb his desire.

'Cheers, Derek.' The landlord set the two fresh pints down and took the crisp £20 note offered to him in exchange. Mozzer waited for the change, turned and headed back to the table where Baggy was sitting. As he went he shot a glance at the table where the two men were sitting. His eyes fixed for a split second with those of the man wearing the light blue shirt.

Lopes quickly looked away, not wanting to draw attention to himself. He grabbed for his pint of shandy and took a long slow drink. Sitting with him was Detective Phil Williams. Williams was based with Lopes at Nottingham. Since the meeting at Billy Davis's house last Monday DI Young had assigned more officers to the case. Detective Williams had worked under DI Young as a spotter in the crowd at Nottingham Forest and had become a favourite with the DI. When DI Young got promoted, Williams was immediately offered a place within the Football Intelligence Unit by way of reward for all his hard work, and he had grabbed the job with both hands. Williams loved the world of the football hooligan. He loved to sit among the lads and eavesdrop on their violence. He loved to spot the faces and then pick them out for the uniform boys to arrest as he sat in the safety of the police control room. Williams felt that he and he alone was cleaning the game up of the filth that threatened to wreck it. Yet when the opportunity arose, down some side alley, or in the back of a police van, Williams would be only too willing to stick the boot in, safe in the knowledge that he could hide behind his police badge.

'They're all in here tonight, Alan. I recognised that lad walking back from the bar. Steven Morris I think his name is.'

'Yes it is, and I think he clocked me looking at him.' Lopes sounded concerned but Williams clearly wasn't.

'Don't worry, Alan. I've spent hours sitting among these idiots. He wouldn't come near you on his own. Anyway we're in a pub, people look, especially southerners.' Williams spoke the words a little too loudly for comfort.

'Keep the level down, will you? He might not fancy a one on one but taking a look around here I don't fancy us two onto 40 or 50.'

'Look, if you act scared then they will suspect something. If you act normal and even give a bit back then they'll leave it. Trust me.'

Lopes took a long, slow look around the bar. On the other side of the room Mozzer sat back down opposite Baggy.

'Quick, look over at the two blokes by the window.'

Baggy turned his head in order to search them out. His eyes fell on the two men. 'What about them?'

'Old Derek reckons they're filth.'

Baggy quickly became more interested. He sounded thoughtful as he checked them. Both men wore blue jeans. One sat wearing a leather bomber jacket over his white buttoned down collar shirt, the other wore a light blue shirt and had a green country jacket draped over the back of his seat.

'Yeah. Judging by the clothes he may well be right there.' He turned to Mozzer. 'What do ya want to do?'

'Well, I'd like to find out.'

'Fair enough.' Baggy turned around again and pulled at the back of Charlie's shirt. Charlie was an expert pickpocket. Although he was straight he could, if he needed to, easily make a living working the tourist areas of the west end. He turned to find out what Baggy wanted.

'See the geezer in the corner wearing the blue shirt? I want you to go and lift his wallet.'

'Why's that then, Baggy?'

'He's annoying me and so I want him to buy us all a beer and find out who he is, that's all.'

'Fair enough.' Charlie put his beer on the table, turned and whispered into Kelly's ear. The two then moved off across the pub towards the table by the window.

Lopes sat nervously by the window. He had heard talk of an attack on a night club south of the river, but nothing about Saturday's expected battle with the Leeds firm. Now he started to feel on edge, as if at any moment the pub would fall silent and every pair of eyes would turn and fix on him. He checked his wrist watch. The time was 10.28 p.m.

'We'll give it ten more minutes then we'll leave, OK?' Williams nodded. 'I need a piss.' Lopes got to his feet and made his way through the crowded bar.

Mozzer clocked the man rise and head off towards the gents. 'Here we go.' Baggy turned to watch as Mozzer followed suit. 'You wait here and I'll see what I can find out.' Quickly he got to his feet and headed off in the same direction.

Over by the window Charlie moved in on the jacket that hung on the back of the seat. Casually he pretended to stretch and look out of the window. He spoke to the man sitting at the table as if to explain his actions.

'Bloody taxi.' He tutted and looked across at Kelly who was now standing beside Detective Williams. 'Should have been here twenty minutes ago, the wanker.'

Kelly began to join the conversation. 'You did order it, didn't ya?'

Charlie's reply was sharp. 'Of course I did you prat.'

Williams sat and watched the conversation take place. Suddenly there was a sharp aching pain down below as Kelly stood upon his foot. He let out a short cry and pulled his foot away.

'Ah fuck. Sorry, mate,' Kelly apologised. Williams' attention was focused on the pain in his foot and upon Kelly's words. Inside he wanted to lash out but he kept calm, bent down and rubbed at the pain.

'It's OK.'

At the other side of the table Charlie had seized the moment. His fingers had been quick to work, plucking the wallet from the second pocket they had entered. Already he was heading back towards the table where his beer and Baggy were waiting.

Meanwhile Mozzer entered the toilet to find Lopes already in mid-flow. He stood at the other end of the urinal and slowly removed his penis from his jeans. Lopes felt a shot of fear shudder down his spine. Mozzer leant forward, placing his hand against the wall in front as if he were drunk. He then begun his act.

'Fuck, I'm pissed.' Mozzer's words were offered as a question. Out of hope Lopes took the bait.

'Yeah. Me too!'

Mozzer knew he was talking bollocks. He tried to gain more information without sounding threatening.

'That's not a London accent. Where you from, mate?'

'Oh I am from the Midlands originally.' Lopes knew he was being questioned and he wanted out. He tried to keep control of the conversation as he finished his piss and put his cock away. In his haste urine trickled down the inside of his jeans. 'I am down here working for a couple of weeks.' Without washing his hands he made for the exit. Mozzer called after him.

'Good luck, then.' As the door closed Mozzer stood upright and shook his head. 'I am just working down here . . . bollocks.'

Charlie returned to the table and handed the prize to Baggy.

'There you go.'

'Nice one.' Baggy opened the brown leather wallet. The first thing to catch his eye was the police identity badge. 'Fuck. Derek was right.' Charlie noticed Baggy's surprised reaction and became interested in who he had just ripped off.

'Who is he, then?'

Baggy shielded the badge from Charlie's view. 'No one, really. Just some ponce.' Sitting inside one of the pockets of the wallet were four £20 notes. Baggy took them out and gave them to Charlie. 'Here you are, go get the beers in.' Charlie was delighted with his reward and forgot all about wanting to know who the man in the corner was.

Detective Lopes returned to his table to find Williams still rubbing away at his foot.

'I think we've been sussed.' He took his jacket from the back of his chair and drew it over his shoulders. He was anxious to leave. 'Come on, let's go.'

Williams seemed more concerned with the pain nagging away at him. 'Some prat just stamped on my foot. It's bloody agony.' He was fishing for sympathy and in no hurry but Lopes was more concerned for his own safety.

'I'll rub it better in the car, just get a fucking move on, will you?' Williams suddenly noticed the urgency in Lopes' voice and shifted into gear.

At the other end of the bar Mozzer sat back down. Before he could say a word Baggy showed him the contents of the wallet.

'Check this out.'

Mozzer looked at the words on the badge.

Detective Alan Lopes
Football Intelligence Unit
Nottingham

'Nottingham.' He looked up at Baggy who then raised his eyebrows. 'What the fuck are they doing down here?' Mozzer was puzzled. The confirmation that they were Old Bill had thrown him for a second. He asked Baggy's advice. 'What do we do now?'

Baggy clocked the two men getting ready to leave.

'Well, we better think quick. Look, they're doing the off.'

Lopes led the way through the crowd towards the front exit. As Williams followed he met Greg coming the other way carrying a full pint. In his eagerness to leave Detective Williams barged past the lad, knocking the pint of beer from his grip. The glass smashed on the floor, spilling the liquid in all directions. Greg was not happy.

'You clumsy fucking idiot.'

Williams continued towards the door and offered only a passing apology. 'Sorry, mate.' For Greg the apology was nowhere near good enough. His anger spat the words out as he followed after the plain-clothes detective.

'OI, YOU WANKER. FUCK "SORRY," GET TO THAT BAR AND ORDER ME ANOTHER FUCKING PINT.'

Across the bar Baggy turned to Mozzer.

'There's your answer.'

Both he and Mozzer rose to watch the spectacle about to take place. Greg grabbed at Williams' shoulder, spinning the man around. The detective tried to brush his arm away and make for the door as a gap opened around the two men. Greg shot out his right arm. His fist smashed into the eye socket like a hammer blow sending the detective flying backwards in the direction of the door. Greg followed his punch, hoping to connect again before his target escaped through the entrance. 'COME BACK 'ERE, YOU PONCE.'

Lopes grabbed his colleague and dragged him onto the street. Williams forgot the ache in his foot as the hot pain of his eye burned stronger. He felt dazed and confused but recognised Lopes' voice and the words shouted in his ear – 'RUN LIKE FUCK' – still made total sense.

The two policemen had about ten yards on the pack that came bursting out of the pub and fear was helping them to run at maximum speed. Some of those giving chase gave up immediately but Greg and Tony wanted more action.

'OI, COME 'ERE, YOU BASTARD.' Tony was closing in on Williams. When the time was right he stuck out his foot and tripped him from behind. Williams' forward motion set him crashing to the pavement. He felt the skin rip from his hand as he hit the concrete and then began to spin and roll over. His direction was halted only when his body crashed into the side of a parked van. Greg shot past Tony and, without breaking his stride, fired a kick straight into the face of the man on the pavement below. The head shot back like that of a toy doll being shaken by a child. It smacked against the wheel of the van and bounced back, ready to be kicked once more. Tony joined in the attack as the two lads from the CBA launched kick after kick at the body on the floor. Williams curled his body tight as thud after thud hit home. His groans seemed to fuel the venom shown by his attackers but eventually his body became numb and everything went black.

Lopes watched the attack from a safe distance. He winced as he witnessed kick after kick. Eventually the attack stopped. The two lads shouted at the body on the floor, turned and headed back towards the pub. As they went they patted each other on the back and started to laugh. When the coast was clear Lopes ran back to help his colleague. He remembered the words of DI Young about involving other areas of the force. He couldn't call the local police as it would break the operation, but once he realised the state Williams was in he summoned an ambulance. This time Williams would have to console himself with the fact that he would have revenge one day – but on this occasion taking a beating, no matter how bad, would unfortunately just have to be part of the job. Lopes felt inside his jacket and the realisation hit home.

'Where's my fucking wallet?' He looked up to see Mozzer turn and re-enter the pub.

24

It was dead on 7.45 a.m. when DI Young entered the room. Detective Lopes followed in behind. The room fell silent as they took up their position facing the 18 officers waiting to be briefed.

'Gentlemen. Thank you for coming this morning and being so prompt.' Bad time-keeping was one of Young's pet hates. Not one of the officers present dared be late for a meeting called by the DI. He continued: 'I believe we all know each other well and so we will crack on. I take it you all know about the incident in London on Thursday night involving Lopes here and Detective Williams, yes?' The assembled crowd murmured back at him. 'Well, his situation has improved but he has been detained at the Royal Free Hospital in London for further tests. By all accounts it was a serious beating he took and so let that be a warning to all of you as you go about your business today. We are not dealing with Mickey Mouse thugs here, these lads are vicious and relentless. Be careful.'

Lopes began to give out folders containing copies of the photographs they had obtained of the gang as Young continued his brief.

'Today is purely for surveillance purposes. Do not get involved with the local plods. Do not get too close to the target. And do not, I repeat, do not get involved with arresting anyone or in any of the fighting we expect to take place. Is that clear?' Once again the officers acknowledged their superior.

'Right. On the folder you will see written the name of the game you are going to attend today. We believe that the hooligans from Stoke, Leeds and our main target, the London hooligans known as the CBA, are all heading for Crewe railway station where they intend to fight each other. What we need to do is to track all three groups. Six of you will go to watch Stoke play at home and monitor the movements of their firm, six will go to monitor the Leeds gang at Coventry, and the rest will go to Aston Villa where City are playing and monitor the CBA. Now the local police know we have officers coming but they do not know what our motives or plans are. They may well have plans of their own for today, I don't know, but ignore any request for information about this operation. Once you have gained entry to the stadium keep yourself to yourself.'

A hand rose at the back of the room. 'Sir?'

'Yes, Beck?'

'What are our main objectives with this operation?'

'Smashing the London hooligan gang. Overall, that is our main objective. They are our main target as they are seen as the top hooligan firm in the country. If we can finish them off then we will send shockwaves through the rest of the hooligan gangs. At this stage the lads from Leeds and Stoke are secondary to this operation. We already have footage of the London lads fighting, but it is not enough to smash the whole firm.'

Another voice spoke up. 'Will we be filming any incidents today?'

'Lopes and I may video at Crewe station, that's all. What you need to do today is watch and learn from the movements of these gangs. I want you to study their organisation, the way they avoid the local police, etcetera. I want you to try and identify the ring leaders, get to know their faces. Unfortunately we need to track all three firms today and that makes it difficult, but it will help us in the long term. Eventually we intend to lay open a trap for the London firm. In order to do that we need to understand how they and the other gangs work.'

DI Young instructed the officers to study the information and photographs he and Lopes had gathered from the trip to London the previous Saturday. As they came to the end of the meeting Detective Lopes addressed the gathering.

'One final word of warning. As you know, I witnessed the horrific attack on Williams the other night.' He pointed towards two enlarged photographs pinned up on the notice board. 'These two lads here are the ones who put one of us in hospital. Unfortunately we don't know either of their names yet.' His voice suddenly took on an aggressive edge. 'Now, I want these bastards. And so any officer coming back with their names gets free beer for the night, on me.'

A cheer filled the room followed by a voice of disapproval. 'That's not fair. I've got to track the Leeds lads.'

'Don't worry, Beck. If I get their names I'll buy you all a pint.'

DI Young broke the banter. 'Right, you all know your orders. Lopes and I will arrive at Crewe Station at approximately 4.30 p.m. but you will relay all movements to us throughout the afternoon as requested. Is that clear?'

An air of excitement filled the room as the officers rose from their seats and headed off towards the canteen. DI Young stayed behind along with Lopes.

'Alan, you must not let the incident in London cloud your judgement. Nothing must get in the way of this operation. I want you with me on this. You're a good officer, but already you have to keep a low profile as they may recognise your face. The only thing we can get from the beating inflicted on Williams is that they could not have suspected the pair of you as being police officers.' Lopes took a deep breath. 'Surely if they had known that they would have left you alone!'

Lopes thought about his lost wallet and identity card. He said nothing. He had tried to convince himself that he had lost his wallet while running from the pub but in reality he knew it had been lifted. Mozzer had sussed him in the toilet and he knew that too. How could he have been so stupid, leaving his wallet unattended like that? A basic rule from training school. Never leave your ID lying around. If the DI found him out then Lopes would be back walking the streets.

'Sorry. I just feel a little guilty about Williams. It was not nice seeing a colleague taking a beating like that and not being able to help, that's all.'

Young patted him on the back. 'I understand.' There was a short silence. 'Come on, Alan, I'll shout you breakfast.' Then they left the room.

25

'Forty-three return tickets to Crewe, please, love.'

'Forty-three?' The ticket woman was obviously surprised at Mozzer's request. 'Are you having a laugh?'

'Am I smiling?' Mozzer paused then, realising the scale of his request, pulled an envelope full of money from his pocket. 'How much, love?'

She raised her eyebrows then went to work. 'Forty-three day returns at £36.50 each.' Her fingers went to work on the keyboard. 'That'll be £1,569.50. I can give you a discount for every twentieth person travelling which will bring that down to £1,496.50.' She looked at Mozzer, expecting him to turn into Jeremy Beadle at any moment.

'Whatever, love. It ain't my money, really, anyway.'

He flicked through the notes before handing over the cash. He then turned to view the concourse of Euston station as she printed out the tickets. He had seen some fantastic battles within the walls of this building. Euston was always top value for fighting. The building generated so much noise that just 30 blokes could make it sound as if a full-scale riot was taking place. Looking around he could see the rest of the lads milling about and stocking up on sandwiches, drinks, papers and the inevitable soft-porn magazines from the top shelf.

'There you go, dear.'

He turned back to the ticket lady. The sight of the money had finally softened her attitude towards him. 'Thank you very much, love. Good luck.' He collected the tickets and headed off to join Baggy over in the food hall. Mozzer sat down beside his right-hand man.

'That's that sorted. One and a half grand, that lot.'

Baggy choked on his coffee. 'Fuckin' hell. You're havin' a bubble, ain't ya?'

'Easy, you ain't paying. Thank the Yo-Yo Club. Anyway, I got a 70 quid discount.'

Baggy still remained unimpressed.

'Ah well, that's all right then.' The talk then turned to what lay ahead. 'You don't reckon we should try and take the Leeds lads out on the way up Birmingham New Street, do ya?'

'No. That place will be crawling with filth – always is. I don't want to risk getting turned over, either. We go to Villa then hook up with the other firms and go to Crewe mob-handed.'

Baggy knew Mozzer was right.

'OK, you're right. We'll need the numbers if Leeds are really going for it.' His mind then turned to the events of Thursday night. 'What do you think those Nottingham Old Bill were up to, Mozzer?'

'I honestly don't know, Baggy. It looks suspect though. I'd have thought they would have lifted Greg or Tony by now, but nothing. Maybe they heard about Leeds coming to have a pop at The George and wanted to suss the place. It could be them they are after, who knows!'

Mozzer tried to sound unconcerned but since Thursday he had thought of little else. He had noticed the dialling code on the card. It was the same as the number he rang when he wanted to talk to the scout and that worried him. At this stage he kept that secret to himself. Baggy would go into panic if he found out his secret and would want to cool everything down for a while until he felt the heat was off. Mozzer didn't want that, not now, not with such a big hit lined up. No, Mozzer would keep that snippet of information to himself.

It was time to round up the rest of the troops and start heading north. At this stage Mozzer wanted to avoid the Leeds firm at all cost and so looked for a train that wasn't stopping at Coventry. He looked at the departure board.

'Watford, Milton Keynes, Birmingham New Street. Platform 11. That's the one.' As the lads headed off down the incline towards the platform Mozzer noticed the other passengers starting to move aside. He got that first buzz of the day. This was what life was about. Football. The CBA. Not giving a fuck. The power kick. The buzz. Mozzer watched his lads laughing and joking, dressed to the nines in their top gear and he started to laugh to himself. He felt like a king. Walking some 20 yards behind were three British Transport Police, the fat one talking into his radio.

'Yes, sir. They are heading off to catch a Birmingham-bound train from platform 11. Do you want us to board the train with them? Over.'

A voice spoke in his ear.

'No, just see them on the train and away. Then they become someone else's problem.'

26

As the train pulled into Watford junction Mozzer noticed the lads from the Hemel City firm. He ran to the door and pressed the button. He shouted down the platform. 'FUCKIN' CITY WANKERS.'

The mob of lads all turned expecting trouble but let out a cheer when they recognised the Londoner's face. They ran up to join the rest of the CBA. All the lads knew each other's names and faces and the banter soon began. All in all 23 lads from Hemel had joined them and so now the firm was looking tasty. Peter Stanard sat down with Mozzer and Baggy.

'Looking good, Mozzer, looking good.'

Mozzer recognised the buzz in his voice.

'Your lot all sweet are they?'

'Top, Mozzer. This lot love it and they know what to expect. Are you tooled-up?'

'Personally, I've got my trusty baby.' Mozzer felt inside his pocket and pulled out his knuckle-duster. He looked at it lovingly, gave it a kiss and spoke to it as if it were his only child. 'I love you.' He placed it upon his fingers and showed it to the others, his voice becoming cocky once more. 'Look at that. It's fucking lovely, that is.' Stanard admired the weapon as Baggy took up the conversation.

'If you like that, you'll love this.' He started to play with two silver rings on his right hand then held his hand out for all to see. Each ring now had four short spikes, one on each corner. Stanard was amazed.

'Fuckin' hell. Where the fuck did you get those mothers from?'

'I had a mate make them for me. Nasty, eh?'

Stanard called over some of his lads. 'Oi, take a look at this, will ya?' He turned back to Baggy. 'Have you used 'em before?'

'Only once, at Arsenal. I don't know how bad the lad was but I was picking out bits of skin for the next hour afterwards. I only bring 'em out for the big ones.'

Stanard remained transfixed.

'Tell you what, I'll give you a onner for the pair. Go on.' Baggy laughed and started to fold the spikes back into their hiding place.

'Fuck off, 100 quid. Put a naught on the end and I might sell you one if you're lucky.'

'A grand, bollocks. OK, tell you what, 100 for one and me bird goes without her birthday present, there you go.'

'Save your money for your bird.' Baggy continued to laugh. 'If you're good I might show you them again later.'

Mozzer came back into the conversation.

'And what about you – tooled-up?'

Stanard reached in his pocket and pulled out a handful of steel bolts. He played with them in the palm of his hand.

'I pinch 'em from work. I tell you, if one of these hits home you know about it and they are easier to explain away than blades and that.' He was also pleased with his weapon. 'All the lads have got them. Do you want some?'

He held out his hand and Mozzer took three for inspection.

'Yeah, nice. Don't mind if I do.'

As the train shot through Hemel Hempstead station Stanard and his lads began to sing.

. . . CITY, 'EMEL, 'EMPSTEAD . . . CITY, 'EMEL, 'EMPSTEAD . . .

27

DI Young walked into the British Transport Police office at Birmingham New Street station and introduced himself and Lopes to the officer behind the desk.

'Ah yes, DI Young, nice to meet you. I am Inspector Willit. Do come through.' After exchanging formalities and ordering coffee the three men sat down. 'So what exactly can I do for you?'

Lopes took hold of the conversation.

'We are monitoring the movements of a group of football supporters from London this afternoon. At this stage we are not sure if they are travelling by train or via the motorways, and so we would like to use your operation headquarters to see if we can pick some of the known faces out.'

'Certainly. Would this be the City firm, the CBA by any chance?'

DI Young was surprised that Willit was so on the ball. 'Yes, it would. Do you know them?'

'This station can become a battleground on most Saturdays. You see, every gang of hooligans in the country passes through here at some stage during the football season. We look at the fixtures a week in advance and that determines how many officers we need on duty. Today could be very nasty and so I have over 20 officers in uniform and another 15 in plain clothes roaming around with the every-day passengers.'

Lopes continued. 'You say today could be particularly nasty. Why is that?'

'Well, you know about the potential of the CBA, otherwise you wouldn't be here. We also expect to have the Leeds lads possibly coming through on their way to Coventry. We hear that the Leeds firm have something arranged elsewhere.' He paused to gauge a reaction then continued. 'Do you know anything about that?' It was a leading question.

Lopes tried to sound surprised as he answered. 'No. Where?'

Inspector Willit lifted his eyebrows and looked across at DI Young. He knew his two guests were taking him for a fool and so he gave nothing away.

'Oh it's only a rumour,' he continued. 'We also have all the local lads from Brum, West Brom, Villa and Wolves to deal with. They will be hanging around at some stage eager to join in if something starts up.' He felt a little let down by the attitude of these so-called colleagues as he rose to his feet. 'Well, gentlemen, you can use the operations room and view the cameras as you wish.' He then took a shot at Young and Lopes. 'After all, we are all on the same side, are we not?'

DI Young felt his cheeks warm. 'Inspector, you have been most helpful. I don't want you to think we are playing games with you.' Willit stopped and waited for more. 'Please let me explain. At this moment an officer of ours is lying in a hospital bed in London after being beaten up on Thursday night and we believe the two men responsible are members of the CBA.'

'Why did you not say?' Once again Willit became helpful. 'I will get some of my men onto the platforms where the London trains arrive and ask them to keep a special lookout for any suspect groups.' Immediately he was on the radio ordering his men. He then showed Young and Lopes the operations room. Once left alone Lopes turned to his superior.

'He seemed to know the rules, all right.'

'Yes, and when that happens you have to give a little more information than you would have liked.'

'Well, I thought you handled him very well.'

'I did. That is why I am the DI and you're my understudy.'

20

The train began to slow and the stomachs began to twitch. Arriving at New Street station could prove to be a very nasty experience as you never knew what kind of welcome committee you were about to receive. The station was one of the most dangerous and exciting stations in the country for those that loved to fight, but this time Mozzer and the lads wanted to go through unnoticed. They disembarked in small groups of no more than five lads together, yet all kept eye contact just in case some of the natives fancied a pop at a few London stragglers.

Upstairs in the operations room Inspector Willit received a call. He turned to Young and Lopes.

'I think we have your target. Look at screen 12.' The two men looked hard. 'They have split into small groups apparently.'

Suddenly Lopes let out an excited shout. 'There. Yes, there they are.' He got right up close to the screen and placed his finger on the face of one man. 'That's one of the bastards that did Williams.' He faced DI Young. 'That's him.'

Young studied the screen. He too became excited.

'That is them, all right. I can see a few of the faces now.'

Willit took over. 'They are making their way over to the correct platform for the Villa train.' He looked at the screen. 'That is quite a mob. I'd say between 50 and 70, wouldn't you?' No one answered. As the camera tracked the gang, uniformed officers began to appear and usher the firm onto the correct platform. DI Young finally broke away from the images being displayed.

'Your men seem to know what they are doing, Inspector.'

'We get a lot of practice. Thankfully the locals seem to have thought twice about having a go at them. It isn't usually that straightforward.'

Down on the platform Mozzer, Stanard and Baggy were pleased to see the police arrive.

'That's handy. We should have this lot with us all the way now and that'll keep us out of trouble.'

Stanard agreed with the main man. 'I tell you what,

Mozzer, I ain't got through there that easy for a long time, I can tell ya.'

They boarded the first train to arrive and headed off to Villa Park.

Up in the operations room DI Young and Lopes thanked their host and made their way down onto the station concourse. As they made their way out of the station, they suddenly stopped short as a deafening noise filled the air.

. . . WE ARE LEEDS, WE ARE LEEDS, WE ARE LEEDS . . .

It seemed things were going totally to plan.

29

Young and Lopes sat in the car outside the station, listened to the football and waited for the calls to come in from their officers out with the various firms. Information had been coming all afternoon. The Leeds firm were out in full force and were already causing trouble. A pub had been taken over and the place smashed up when the local police had tried to clear it out before the game kicked off. The officers with them estimated a hard core of around 200 hooligans with at least the same again on the fringes. At Stoke the officers were finding it harder to estimate the numbers but had picked up on rumours that Leeds were expected to visit after the game. Also present at the Stoke game were the group of hooligans from Dundee and they seemed to be at the centre of things as much as the Stoke lads were themselves. At Villa the CBA were just one of around 15 firms of City lads numbering anything from as little as ten and up to 50. One thing was for sure – Crewe station was not going to be a nice place to visit at any time between 5.30 p.m. and 7 p.m. that evening.

The two listened as the football results came through. Villa and City had drawn 1–1. Leeds had also drawn, only for them it was 2–2. Stoke had beaten Norwich 2–0. Suddenly the crowds from the local match at Gresty Road started to filter past the vehicle and into the station.

'I pray for this lot that they don't get caught up here later.'

That was the thing that DI Young hated most about the violence surrounding football. These people were just innocent fans out enjoying the sport they loved. Yet it was likely that at some stage during their supporting lives they would come across the likes of the CBA and have their faces smashed. That was why he was here now. He had to do the best he could for these people. He had to try and smash the CBA. They sat and waited and then a line of police began to pass the car, escorting the visiting Swindon supporters back to the station. They watched as a small group of local so-called hard nuts, no more than 18 years old, passed on the other side of the road, abusing the Swindon fans as they went. Lopes cracked a joke to relieve the boredom.

'Do you reckon they'll be up for it later?'

DI Young laughed. 'I think a clean change of underwear would soon be required if they knew what was heading this way right now, don't you?'

'Nappies, more like.'

Thirty minutes passed then the mobile rang.

'Hello. Holt here. The CBA are on the Crewe train now. We should be arriving within the next half hour. It's definitely happening at this end.'

The DI replied. 'Good work, Holt. Stick with them but keep your head down, OK?'

Soon the phone rang again. The Leeds firm were also moving their way. Finally the call from Stoke brought some relief – their hooligans were staying in their local pubs hoping the Leeds firm would come to them.

'Well, Alan, that's some good news at least. Now we get to see what we're up against.'

DI Young took the bag containing the video camera from the back seat of the car and the two policemen headed off into the building. Crewe station was an impressive building, an engineering masterpiece. Young took a look at the innocent travellers swarming across the platform. There were old people, young people, families.

'I wish I could make an announcement and clear this place of all these decent people.' He looked across to see two of the station staff joking with each other, totally oblivious to the danger they were about to find themselves in.

'Yeah, I agree.' Lopes had the same fears. 'We should clear this place and let the bastards fight it out until they kill each other. Then all we have to do is pick up the pieces and throw them in a hole where they belong.'

DI Young nodded in agreement then the pair headed off to get a last cup of coffee.

30

The motorbike pulled up and the rider climbed off. He went to the top box at the back of the GPZ 750 and removed a small holdall. He checked his watch. 5.58 p.m. . . . *Thank fuck* . . . Billy Davis had made it with time to spare. He had sat at home going over and over the possibilities of getting followed, of getting spotted and of getting arrested. But he couldn't stay away. He had decided to stand at the end of one of the quiet platforms and latch on to some of the train-spotters who flocked to the big junction station. There he would be safe from the prying eyes of the police who would most certainly be more interested in every other type of person travelling through rather than those with the sad hobby of collecting train numbers. In the bag was his video camera. The CBA versus Leeds, that was too good to miss. Fuck Lopes and DI Young. He removed his crash helmet and replaced it with a woollen hat. He then pulled his scarf up over his mouth. Only bikers could get away with being dressed that way on such a beautiful sunny afternoon. He bought a platform ticket from the counter and then headed off to join the saddos.

31

The carriage on the train was crammed solid. All the other passengers who until recently had occupied these seats had long since moved away from the mass of lads clearly out looking for trouble. Mozzer checked his fellow City fans. The CBA and the Hemel City lads had been joined by at least another 70 lads from around the south-east. Smaller mobs from Bromley, Hitchin and Kingston had helped to bolster the firm to around 150, and these were all top boys. The train ground to a halt and the City supporters disembarked. The adrenalin was rushing through the firm. You could almost feel the electricity in the air as all eyes checked the station. Over on one of the far platforms a small gang of local lads witnessed the arrival of the London firm and soon made a hasty exit away from the danger.

Up on the walkway the two policemen looked down. Lopes was first to speak.

'Bloody hell, look at that lot.' It was an awesome sight. He went for the video camera but DI Young pulled him up.

'Not now, Lopes. They're heading our way, it's too obvious.'

Lopes looked on. 'This is fucking dangerous. If I get recognised I am dead meat.' He bent down pretending to search something out from within the bag.

The firm moved up the stairs in a sinister silence, looking like a pack of rats searching out prey as worried travellers moved aside. Within seconds the lads seemed to disappear as they split into smaller groups and stood waiting. Those who had seen them arrive knew of their presence but any new travellers coming into the station would just see groups of lads hanging around waiting to catch their trains back to the warmth of their own homes. How wrong they were.

'Let's head down towards one of the platforms and wait at the end with the trainspotters. We should be out of the way there.'

DI Young's suggestion was music to Lopes's ears, and the two headed off down the stairs that were just moments ago crawling with football hooligans.

Mozzer and the rest of his firm made their way towards one of the station cafes and took up residence inside. The girl behind the counter took a sharp intake of breath as the firm entered.

Mozzer sorted himself a position by the window that gave him an excellent view of the station. Over on the platform opposite he could see Stanard and his boys keeping their own lookout. Up on the stairs he could see the lads from north London doing their best to look angelic, and on the platform outside he could see another small mob of City lads bouncing, buzzing, ready. As every train pulled in, the buzz shot through their veins. The lads bought food and drink to calm their nerves. Clarkie stood at the counter ordering tea as the door to the cafe opened and in walked five lads. The girl behind the counter placed the polystyrene cup down in front of Clarkie.

'That'll be 99 pence, please.'

'You got any sugar, love?' Suddenly, from behind, Clarkie heard a voice.

'Ah look, lads, a Cockney wanker.' The accent was thick. The cafe fell silent. Somehow the lad had failed to notice the rest of the 'travellers' sitting inside the warm cafe. Clarkie's back went tight. Slowly he looked over his shoulder. He was greeted by the grinning face of the northerner aged about 28 and his four mates, younger but just as ugly. He took a step back. He looked ready for action, his eyes fixed solid on Clarkie's face. His mates were ready for the door, their faces full of fear.

'Are you talking to me?' Clarkie was almost laughing as the words came out.

'I don't see any other southern shites around, do you?'

'Eh, I think you might be wrong there, sonny.' Clarkie's fist tightened, ready to fire.

Mozzer jumped up from his seat by the window. 'Clarkie, leave it.'

The motormouth suddenly looked around. His eyes picked up on the crowd staring at him. Visibly he began to shrink. He looked back at Clarkie, then at his mates trying to back away. The Londoner wanted to smash his face but knew he had a much more impressive target heading his way in the shape of the Leeds firm and so resisted the challenge. He grabbed the lad by the front of the shirt.

'Listen, you cock-sucking northern cunt, if I weren't waiting for something a little more impressive to arrive then I'd rip your fuckin' arms off and ram them right up your fuckin' arse. YOU HEAR?' The lad said nothing and so Clarkie aggressively shouted a prompt. 'I SAID, D'YOU HEAR, FUCK-HEAD?' This time he nodded. 'Yeah. Yeah, sorry, pal, I fucked up.' Clarkie released his grip, pushing the lad away at the same time. He fell against the side of the counter. The girl looked on, locked by fear.

'Yeah, you fucked up all right, *pal*.' He then focused in on the shirt the lad was wearing. It had the badge of County upon it. Again he laughed. 'You're out of your league, son. Get the shirt off.'

'What?'

Again Clarkie became annoyed as the rest of the CBA watched.

'I said, GET THAT FUCKIN' SHIRT OFF.'

Without hesitation the lad lifted the shirt over his head and handed it to Clarkie. He snatched at the shirt then threw it on the ground. Slowly he undid the buttons on his 501s and removed his penis from his pants. The lad pleaded with him not to do it as cheers and laughter filled the rest of the cafe.

'Please don't, mate, please.'

Clarkie strained for the first few drops of liquid. More fell upon the shirt, then more, then a constant flow. Clarkie said nothing, just stared at the shirt then at its owner. He finished his piss, shook himself dry and replaced his tackle. He smiled.

'There. That's better. Now put it on.'

'Oh, come on, mate, you made your . . .'

Clarkie suddenly turned into a madman, his patience running out. 'PUT IT FUCKIN' ON.'

The lad slowly bent down and picked up the sopping garment. He pulled the shirt over his head, the material sticking to his naked skin, his hair wet with the fresh urine. Clarkie was calm once more.

'That's it. Now let that be a lesson to ya.' He then turned back to the girl behind the counter. 'Right, where's that sugar?' She stood transfixed by the Londoner, her hand held forward, two sachets of white sugar in her palm. 'It's all right, love, I only need the one.' He took the sachet, turned and headed off towards Mozzer and the table by the window.

The northerners stood by the counter frightened to move, one dripping wet as a shower of paper plates and polystyrene cups flew in their direction amid howls of laughter and taunts.

Tony patted Clarkie on the back as he went. 'You're fucking sick you are, Clarkie.'

32

Billy couldn't believe his eyes as he looked across at the couple walking slowly up the platform on the opposite side of the tracks. His mind started racing. . . . *Fuck me, no . . . It's Young and Lopes . . . No . . .* He turned away and moved off to gain some cover behind one of the station name signs.

Back in the cafe the atmosphere was getting tense.

Suddenly Mozzer noticed the City lads on the stairs straighten. He sat up.

'Hang on, lads, this could be it.' Everybody in the cafe rose to their feet. Then came the sign. The lads on the stairs started to back up onto the walkway. One of the lads gestured to Stanard and his lads. He then turned and gave Mozzer the sign. This was it. Mozzer turned to his troops, the rush banging through his body. He shouted at the top of his voice. 'THIS IS IT, LADS. LET'S FUCKIN' DO IT.'

The doors of the cafe burst open as the firm swarmed out and onto the platform. Stanard and his boys were already at the top of the stairs?

Mozzer turned to Baggy. 'We wait here. Once the train pulls out we steam across the tracks at 'em. They don't even know we're here yet.'

'What if they can't hold the stairs?'

'The Leeds lads ain't got a fucking chance with those nuts and bolts raining down on 'em. No, we do it my way, Baggy.'

Suddenly the noise became deafening.

. . . UNITED . . . UNITED . . .

Mozzer could hear the noise of stampeding feet. He looked up at Stanard and his lads. Suddenly they let go a rain of steel. He watched as they moved forward. They were obviously driving the Leeds firm back but soon they ran out of ammunition and the real fighting began. The train slowly began to pull away. The sound of glass smashing and innocent people screaming mixed in with the hate-filled cries of Stanard and his boys as they steamed down the stairs and into their enemy. They were backed up by more City lads. The CBA were waiting, dying to join the action. Bouncing, shouting. Finally the train was gone and Mozzer caught his first sight of the Leeds firm. His stomach knotted. There were hundreds of them, but he didn't wait. The CBA poured across the track and into battle. The platform was already littered with the bodies of people hit by the flying steel Stanard and his lads had fired off. Some were Leeds fans, some were innocent people caught in the wrong place at the wrong time. Mozzer didn't care about them now, he didn't have time to care.

The main lads of the Leeds firm had been deserted by the hangers-on. Mozzer knew that would make others lose their bottle as well and now they were left with only the real hard core. The City lads darted in with fists and boots flying, but the Yorkshiremen were not ready to retreat and were beginning to hold their own when they caught sight of Mozzer and the boys heading across the tracks. The attack had certainly taken them by surprise. They were desperate to regroup but the Londoners' attack was relentless as they began to force them further and further back down the platform towards where DI Young and Detective Lopes were standing.

Mozzer found his first victim. His boot hit hard into the kidneys, making the lad buckle and wince in pain. As he bent forward Mozzer was on him like a shot and brought the side of his trusty tool down hard upon the back of his neck. The lad crumbled and fell to the floor. Kelly followed in behind, kicking hard. Then Doug, kicking, kicking, kicking. The lad was finished. Motionless. Mozzer moved forward. He wanted more. His mind worked into a frenzy as he ran forward screaming. 'COME ON . . . *BASTARDS*.'

DI Young began to panic and for the first time lost his cool composure. 'We're right in the fucking firing line here. STOP BLOODY FILMING AND RUN FOR IT.' Lopes was lost in his duty. The violence had taken him over and he wanted to capture every moment. Suddenly the retreating Leeds mob were around him.

Mozzer picked his next target. The Yorkshireman wasn't ready to turn and run. As he jostled backwards he beckoned

Mozzer on. His teeth were gritted as the words barked out from him. 'Come on, you southern cunt. *COME ON.*'

Mozzer moved within striking distance but his opponent was quick. He felt the dull, hard thud hit home. His world went black then shot back into focus. Instinctively he moved back and shook his head. Then the searing pain shot from his eye and through his body. A boot flashed past his groin, missing its target by inches. The Yorkshireman had won the battle, now it was time to leave as the rest of his lads got pushed further away. He turned and was on his toes. Danny shot past the dazed Mozzer at full speed. He had seen the punch land and wanted revenge. He closed in on his prey and brought the cosh down on the back of his head. The Yorkshireman's legs buckled. He tried to keep going, slowly falling. Danny hit him again. He fell to his knees, then slumped forward. Mozzer came around and saw Danny going to work.

'*Bastard.*' He ran forward and grabbed the head of the man now groaning on the floor. With one hand he gripped his cheeks and turned his face so that he was staring directly into his eyes. He smiled

'Have this, you cunt.' He fired the knuckle-duster into his face. The nose shattered, skin ripped and deep red crimson flowed across his face. One shot was enough. Mozzer let go his grip and got to his feet. Danny was already homing in on his next target, the man with the video camera. He came at him from the side, his right boot sweeping the man's feet from under him and sending him crashing to the ground. The camera spun away across the concrete. Lopes felt his shirt rip as he hit the ground, then his skin began to sting. He tried to scurry away, screaming.

'LEAVE ME ALONE, LEAVE ME ALONE.'

Danny went after the camera, picked it up and stuffed it under his polo shirt. That would fetch a nice price down The George. Lopes had gained just enough time to get himself clear. He then slipped, which held him up just enough for Greg to launch a size nine right up his arse.

'GO ON, YA FUCKER.' The rocket lifted Lopes to his feet and sent him on his way.

Over on the platform opposite Billy Davis captured the moment. He didn't know it but he was shouting loudly, egging the City lads forward. *'Go on, go on, lads.'* The rest of the trainspotters were long gone, fearing for their safety. Now Billy better do the same.

The City lads had done the business. Stanard was rushing his bollocks off on the violence. He called across to Mozzer. 'RE-FUCKIN'-SULT, MOZZER, SON.' The cry went up and filled the air.

. . . CITY . . . CITY . . . CITY . . .

Mozzer called back. 'We better do the off. This place will be crawling with Old Bill any minute.' They took one last look at the Leeds lads running down the track away from their attackers. It had been the perfect hit.

Mozzer spotted a train pulling in on one of the south-bound platforms. 'JUMP THAT TRAIN. LET'S GET THE FUCK OUT OF 'ERE.'

The City boys piled into the carriages full of Joe Public. The train began to pull away, taking them past the Leeds fans dotted along the side of the track. They taunted the Yorkshiremen through the windows. A shower of stones flew towards them, then a sleeper bracket smashed through the window sending glass flying inside the packed carriage now occupied by Mozzer and his lads. A woman screamed and children started crying. The City boys continued with their torrent of abuse. Within minutes the Leeds fans had given up the chase and were out of sight. The carriage was full of song as the everyday passengers tried to move away to another part of the train, desperate to avoid any further violence. Mozzer was still full of rage, full of the adrenalin pumping through him. He glared at the ordinary people as they gathered their things and moved past him. He began to wonder. How did they get *their* buzz? What excited their empty little lives? He checked the faces of the lads around him. His lads, their voices racing, full of it. They were not ordinary. They belonged to something, something they would die for. He took a deep breath, raised his fist in the air and then shouted at the top of his voice.

. . . C-I . . . C-I-T . . . C-I-T-Y, CITY . . .

The rest of the army joined his chant.

Baggy jumped onto his back. 'We fucked 'em, son. We fuckin' slaughtered 'em.'

Moments later Stanard came to join them. 'Look, we better spread out. Chances are that when we get to New Street the pigs will swarm over us like flies on shit.' He was right and so Mozzer took his lads and told them to spread themselves out, just in case.

Back at the station DI Young finally caught up with Lopes. 'Are you OK?'

Lopes lost his cool and forgot rank for a while.

'No thanks to you. Fucking cheers.' He was rubbing his elbow. 'Fuck those bastards.' Young let the pop at him go as the pair were joined by the rest of the undercover team. In the background the sound of police sirens grew louder.

'We better get out of here quick. I don't want us involved with the local police. Meet you all back at the station.' The team moved off as Young turned his attention back to Lopes. 'Where's the camera?'

Lopes, still smarting from his beating, walked off towards the car, now rubbing his hip.

'Fucked if I know.'

Outside the station the riot vans screeched to a halt as the motorbike headed off past them in the opposite direction. As the warm night air hit his face Billy Davis began to roar with laughter.

33

The train ground to a halt. The platform was lined with uniformed officers ready to make sure their was no repeat of the violence that had taken place at Crewe. Inspector Willit joined some of his officers on the train as they tried to search out some of the main ringleaders. Deep down he knew he had no chance of making an arrest and that his actions were just for show, but put on a show he must. You could have heard a pin drop as the officers made their way down the train. The faces of grown, violent men trying to look as innocent as choirboys filled his vision. Eventually he made his way off the train and back onto the platform. He watched as the train slowly began to move. As he turned to head back to the operation room the wall of sound started.

. . . CITY . . . CITY . . . CITY . . .

He looked around to see Mozzer and his lads leaning out of every window, taunting him and his fellow policemen.

34

The trip back to the police station in the car with Lopes had been a long and silent journey. Once in the incident room, DI Young addressed his officers and asked them to give up all the information they had gained during the day.

'Now that we have all witnessed It at first hand, we must all acknowledge the fact that these lads are highly organised. I don't think we can dilly-dally over this any longer, we must move fast if we are going to smash them.'

Beck called out from the back of the room. 'What's the intention? Do we try and infiltrate them or what?'

'No, Beck. That is too dangerous for the individual officer and has proven difficult for other forces in the past. Also it is too time-consuming. No, the only way is to gain as much video evidence as possible over the coming weeks and then set the firm up.'

'You must have gained some good footage today, sir, surely.'

DI Young looked over at Lopes, then back to Beck.

'No. No, we didn't. But the information we did gather will help us to target certain individuals and so today has been a great success. Well done all of you.'

Officer Babb asked a final question. 'Sir, how do you intend setting the firm up?'

'Well, as I told you this morning we have got an informant. He will now play a major part in that side of things.' He looked back at Lopes, who was still rubbing his hip. 'Won't he, Lopes?'

'Too bloody right he will.'

35

The train arrived back at Euston on time. The firm soon filled the station platform as the rest of the passengers held back, thankful that the yobs had now left their world. They marched as a triumphant army would march, up the ramp and onto the concourse. It was an impressive sight. Once more they began to sing, announcing their arrival back home. What a fantastic city London was. Mozzer had suggested a pub crawl around the west end to finish the day off, in which Stanard and all the other lads were only too happy to take part. After a quick food stop they marched off towards the Underground and caught a tube on the Northern line down to Leicester Square.

The firm soon drove the original occupants of The Porcupine pub out as they took up residence. The landlord didn't mind, he knew the City lads well and now had a pub full of serious drinkers rather than soppy, fuck-witted tourists. Mozzer stood outside watching the girls walk past. Could there be any better place to be than in London on a hot summer night? He didn't think so. The whole world came to this city and they all passed by this particular pub. He watched the lads teasing the women, women from every country in the world. Stanard placed another pint in his hand.

'There you go, son.'

'Look around you, Peter. Is this the dog's bollocks or what?' The pair took the moment in.

'Yeah, I suppose it could be worse, Mozzer.' They continued drinking.

Slowly the numbers began to fall as the lads from the other areas began to make their way back to their home towns. It was time to make a move. Pinhead and Tony were off clubbing once more but Mozzer wasn't in the mood for it this week and so he, Baggy and Danny made their way back to The George. As they sat on the Central line train, Danny started playing with the video.

'What a result this was lads.'

Mozzer sat forward. 'Was that the one from that trainspotter on the platform?'

'Yeah. Bastard was filming every move. Actually it might be well worth watching when I get home.'

Mozzer looked at Baggy. 'Yeah, it well might be.'

Danny took his eye away from the view-piece. 'You want to buy it, Baggy?'

'Got one, Dan. I've got everything, you should know that.'

'Worth a try. What about you, Mozzer?' He went off on the sales pitch. 'Tell ya what, as it's you I'll do ya a deal!'

Mozzer started laughing at the wide boy and shook his head. 'You prat.' He offered the others a question. 'Did either of you get a look at that bloke? He looked familiar to me.'

Baggy shook his head. 'No, can't say I did.'

'No, me neither.' Mozzer sat back and tried to place the face in his mind. 'Funny that.' He paused. 'Ah well, maybe he just had one of those faces, then.' He played the image over and over in his mind. 'Danny, I am sure you'll find some mug who'll 'ave it, but don't lose that video right. I need to see it.'

36

The ring of the doorbell had taken Billy by surprise. He wasn't expecting any visitors this morning and so despite the time being 10.37 a.m. he was still in his dressing gown. He peered through the curtains to see Detective Lopes waiting with one other man.

'What the fuck does he want?' Billy said the words out loud. He felt the nerves take hold as he opened the door. Lopes stood there grinning back at him, looking cocky.

'Ah good, Davis, you're in.' He sounded on edge and made his way forward, pushing past Billy. 'May we come in?' The other officer was Beck, although Lopes made no attempt at an introduction. Beck pushed Billy back and slammed the door behind him.

Billy was pissed off at the forced entry. 'You got no right barging in here. What's the problem?'

Lopes spun around, fighting to control his anger. 'YOU'RE THE FUCKING PROBLEM, DAVIS. YOU.'

Billy backed against the wall, at two onto one the odds were not in his favour. Lopes placed his hand on the wall by Billy's face and moved his forehead forward so that it was just inches from Billy's nose.

'Listen, you no-good streak of piss. When all this is over I am going to have you, you hear me? One day there won't be no nice DI Young looking out for you, Davis, and then I'll have your arse. Now me and my colleague here would like you to start giving up names now before I lose my temper.'

Billy knew this little visit was not noted down on the police roster. He had been here time and time again. The two filth had come to put the shits up him without Young knowing and in reality they could do nothing.

Billy called Lopes' bluff. 'I tell you what, Lopes, why don't you do me over now?' He looked at Beck. 'Go on. You an' old sperm count 'ere, go for it, go on. Then we will see what Young has to say about you fuckin' with his chief grass.'

Lopes shot his right hand forward, forcing the palm against Billy's forehead. His skull cracked against the wall behind. He then fought with himself to regain control of his aggression.

'YOU MOUTHY SHIT.' He knew Billy was right. He drew on his throat, pulling up thick, green phlegm into his mouth. He pouted his lips then spat in Billy's face. 'That's for you, Billy.' He then shot a look up the hallway. He grabbed the front of Billy's gown and dragged him in the direction of the spare bedroom. 'Here, hold him here.' He shoved Billy at Beck, who took a tight grip of the Londoner's arm. Lopes leant his back against the wall opposite the door then launched his boot forward. It crashed into the wood. A crack shot through the air as splinters flew out from the frame. Lopes attacked again and the door shot open. All Billy could do was stand and watch. Lopes entered the room and took the same deep breath he had taken on his last visit.

'Well, well, Mr Davis. What have we here then?' He pointed to the cuttings that were sitting in a tray underneath the window. Billy said nothing. Lopes casually walked over to the plant pots and brought his full weight down upon them. 'Oh I am sorry, Billy. I am a clumsy fucker.' Lopes felt calm. He was king at this moment, loving every second and in full control. Billy watched him as he wrecked his factory. Lopes moved towards one of the cabinets over by the far wall and opened the door. The ultra-violet light burst forward followed by the warm air. Lopes turned to Billy.

'This is nice, Billy. I never knew you were such a keen gardener.'

Billy moved to try and finally wipe the gob from his face. Beck tugged hard at his arm. Lopes then moved one arm to the back of the cabinet and set the unit crashing forward. Weed, soil and glass spread itself across the floor as an almighty crash sent shudders through the flat. Lopes moved to the other cabinet. Still king.

'And what about this one, Billy?' He brought that crashing down as well. He then turned his attention towards the timer switches sitting neatly in the plug sockets. The heel of his boot cracked the plastic and demolished the clock faces. It was a job done. Finally he checked the small chest of drawers, only to find four glass jars full of top-quality buds. He turned to Billy. 'Now, Billy, let us see if you tell DI Young about all this, shall we? I think not.' He took one of the jars and placed it under his arm. 'Shame to waste all of this, eh, Billy?' Lopes then walked from the room, up the hallway and back out into the morning sunshine.

Beck shook Billy free. 'Be seeing you, Mr Davis.' Then he too was on his way.

Billy stood gazing at the wreckage. Inside he felt amazingly calm . . . 'FUCKING BASTARD.' . . . He headed off to the bathroom and washed his face repeatedly in order to remove any trace of the spit from his person. He tightened the belt on his gown, walked into the front room and turned on the television. He picked up the video remote control and pressed the play button. On the screen flashed the images of Saturday. He knelt down and shoved his hand underneath his armchair. His fingers worked through the lining and found their prize. He got back to his feet and turned to face the television just in time to see Lopes getting kicked. He lifted the revolver up, and holding his arms out stiff in front of him fired off an imaginary bullet.

'Bye bye, *Mr* Lopes.'

Then Billy began to laugh.

37

Mozzer took the beer being offered by Tony and sat down on the back doorstep to watch the rest of the lads fuck about. Danny was busy showing off his new toy, trying desperately to get everyone and anyone to speak into the camera. He had watched the footage Lopes had shot before being attacked over and over. It was good. The firm appeared mad, even evil. Mozzer had been caught directly in shot as he broke the nose of his victim. You could see the blood spurt from the wound as the metal hit the skin and smashed the cartilage. The image brought a smile to Mozzer's face.

He had studied the video, looking for clues as to the identity of the man he had seen taking the film but had seen nothing that could enlighten him. Just boots, fists and blood. Terry from Sheffield had rung earlier that day to congratulate him. News of the hit was all over Yorkshire. The Leeds firm were licking their wounds. He also informed Mozzer that fighting had broken out amongst the Leeds fans as those who stayed and fought took their beating out on those who ran. As for the Stoke mob, well they had been waiting all night and the Leeds firm hadn't shown. Today they would probably find out why. Mozzer's firm were sitting back at the top of the tree and it brought a smile to his face as he soaked up the sun. His daydream was suddenly broken.

'You OK? Laughing away to yourself there.' Julie stood before him. She looked fantastic.

'Oh yeah. Sorry, love, I was miles away.'

'I noticed.' She parked herself down beside him, placing her hand on his thigh to steady herself. As she settled, her hand moved closer towards his groin before she finally pulled it away. A pulse shot through his body. The tight fitting T-shirt showed her shape to full effect, the white shorts hugging her hips. Mozzer looked up at the sky.

'Great day for a barbecue.'

He felt uneasy at the tension building up inside him. 'Yeah, lovely. Listen, about last week, I am sorry I snapped.'

'That's OK. Understandable, really.'

He tried to change the subject. 'Ossie looks much better.'

'Oh he's all right.' She sounded unconcerned, then continued. 'Listen, why don't you come round for a chat sometime this week? I haven't had you to myself for ages.' The comment made Mozzer turn to face her. She fixed him with a deep, long stare. 'Ossie's off to his mate's in Wales for two days to pick up some gear. I'll be left all alone.' The stare continued.

'What about the others, they'll be here to look after you.'

'Not during the day, they won't. They're all out at work.' She smiled. He found himself returning the gesture. She took the beer from his hand and took a long slow mouthful before passing the can back to him. 'You wouldn't want to have me here all on my own now, would you, Mozzer? You never know what might happen.' He could feel the rise taking place in his groin as his blood began to rush through him. She rose to her feet. Standing before him she placed her glare upon the bulge in his trousers. 'That's nice.'

She then turned and walked away. Mozzer stayed put, watching her as she moved among her guests. Once again his thought process was shattered as he felt a hand come to rest upon his head. He looked up to see Ossie making his way out from the kitchen. The sight brought him to his senses.

'All right, son?'

'Sweet, Mozzer.' He took a drink from the bottle of wine he was carrying. 'That video, man! Nasty. I wish I could have been there.' He took more drink. 'And that smack you gave that guy. Fuckin' hell, that was a beauty.'

Mozzer smiled up at him. He knew that Ossie was telling the truth. He really did wish he could have been there. Ossie would have loved the chance to run with the pack and stick the boot in where it hurt.

'Next time, Ossie. You'll be there next time, son.'

He patted Ossie's leg and the lad headed off to take the piss out of Danny and his filming technique. He looked back at Julie and shook his head. She didn't understand. No woman could. Ossie was part of the firm, one of his top boys. It didn't matter how much Mozzer fancied her, or how hard she came on to him, the lads from the CBA came first. Julie was Ossie's bird, end of story.

38

This time Billy was expecting the visit. It had been little over 24 hours since Lopes and his monkey had wrecked the flat but he had managed to clear up the mess and even salvage some of his plants. Once again Detective Hunt accompanied DI Young and Lopes.

DI Young explained the purpose of the visit. 'Right, Billy. First off, the information you gave us about Saturday was spot on, which is good, now I know I can trust you as far as that is concerned.'

'Well, thank you.' Billy's words stank of sarcasm.

'Now we need to level with each other.' He paused as Billy lit up a cigarette. 'You see, Billy, like Lopes here, I have now come to the conclusion that you do in fact know more about the lads involved here than you are currently letting on. However, I am sure you have worked out that I am in a difficult situation. I will not take you for a mug, Billy, if you do the same for me. We both know that if I were to do what Lopes suggests and take you down to London then your face, and our operation, would be broken. Agreed?'

Billy filled his cheeks with smoke then blew it in the direction of Lopes. 'Ah sorry.' He waited for Young to continue.

'It would seem that your main use to me is in obtaining information via the phone and then setting up your, shall we say, "friends". Now, once again, you may ask how I intend to do that. Yes?' Once again Billy remained unmoved. 'As you know already, we cannot trace your contact's mobile, but we can record all the calls that come into and go out from this flat. Hunt here is going to install a permanent recording device for me. What I want you to do is call me whenever your contact phones in. Is that clear?'

Billy finally nodded an acknowledgement.

'Now, Billy, one last thing. You may well think you have me by the balls at this moment in time but just to make you think again I would like you to take a look at this.' DI Young handed Billy a small leaflet. On the paper was printed a photograph of Billy along with his name, address and phone number. At the very top above the picture were the words

THIS IS THE CITY SCOUT YOU'VE ALL BEEN LOOKING FOR

Billy couldn't believe his eyes. DI Young finished his lecture.

'Billy, we know where you drink and who you talk to. Now, if one of my officers comes around here and finds a message you have forgotten to pass on to me then I will personally see that a quantity of these leaflets get placed in the correct hands.' He stared at Billy, who had been left dumbstruck. 'Billy, do we have an understanding here?'

Eventually the Londoner nodded.

'Good.'

Detective Hunt went to work on installing the equipment while DI Young headed to the toilet. Lopes took his chance.

'Not so fucking mouthy today, eh, Billy?' Leaning forward he started to mock his host. 'That draw you grew. Good stuff. Shame you're out of business now.'

Billy sprung back to life. He looked up. 'Lopes, you're a wanker, a prize cock.' Billy sucked in his cheeks and returned the favour Lopes had done him the day before. The spit hit his forehead. Lopes jumped up ready to go for Billy. The noise of the chair flying back alerted Hunt.

'What the fuck?'

Lopes managed to control himself as Billy remained unfazed.

'Steady, Mr Lopes. You'll do yourself an injury carrying on like that.'

'I'll do you a fucking injury, Davis.' He pulled the chair back, sat down and took a tissue from his pocket with which to wipe away the saliva. In his head, Billy was living out the moment when his day would come. Yes, he would play DI Young's game, but for one reason only – it would bring that day closer.

39

The week had seemed to drag like no other. It often felt like that to Mozzer when coming down off such a big high. He had re-lived the events of Crewe station over in his mind many times, as had most of the other lads who had rung him during the week in order to talk about it. As he walked from his car towards The George his mind was beginning to look forward to another weekend of violence and the home game with Newcastle United at The Manor.

He entered the bar to a resounding cheer.

. . . LEADER . . . LEADER . . .

As ever the lads took the piss but the message was not lost in the joke. It was the first time they had all been together since the hiding they had given Leeds the previous week and the lads knew that it was down to the planning of Mozzer that they owed their victory. Once again he had manoeuvred them into the right place at the right time and so tonight the beers were on them. He took up residence at his favourite table.

'How's it hanging, son?'

'Sweet, Baggy. Sweet.'

'Danny showed me that video from last week. You're a nasty man, Mr Morris. Nasty.' He started to laugh but noticed that Mozzer's mind seemed elsewhere. 'You all right?'

'Yeah, yeah, no worries. Just thinking about Saturday, that's all.'

'What – Newcastle? They'll turn up all right, always do. I can't wait.' He finished the remains of his pint.

'It's not Newcastle I am thinking about, it's Leeds.'

Baggy got to his feet ready to head for the bar. 'Fuck Leeds. We won't be seeing those wankers for a while. Not after last week.'

'I ain't so sure, Baggy.' He looked up.

Baggy could see the anxiety in his face and sat back down. 'What, have you heard something?' He too was now concerned.

'No, no, nothing like that. It's just they're down at Arsenal Saturday, remember? That was when they were intending to hit us.'

'Yeah, and?'

'We made them look second rate last week. The whole country knows that, and so they need to get a result back.'

'Look, Mozzer, Leeds have been second rate for a few years now. They started to make all sorts of noises and so last week we fucked 'em. Forget Leeds, Mozzer. They're out of the race again, son. We saw to that last week.' He paused awaiting a response but none came forward. 'Fuck me, Mozzer you should know the rules better than anyone. Last week we fucked their reputation big time. That's the name of the game, son, and you know it. I tell you, we won't be seeing those twats again for a few years. Now chill out, for fuck's sake'

'I know what you're saying but I've just got a feeling that's all. What do you say we send a couple of the lads up to Kings Cross on Saturday? Just to scout the place.'

Baggy shrugged his shoulders. 'Well, it wouldn't harm, would it? And if it stops me from having to look at your sour face all night then, yeah, it's a good idea.' There was a short silence. 'Mozzer. Leeds won't be up for it, believe me.'

'Yeah.'

Mozzer's response was still not convincing and so Baggy gave up. He pointed to Mozzer's half-full glass. 'You want another pint while I am there?'

'Yeah, go on then. I think I need it.'

40

DI Young had spent all week picking the right men for the job. Briefings had taken place every day as he discussed and finalised his plans for trapping the firm. This Saturday he and his team would once again track their movements, only this time it would be in London and on their home turf. He needed to be certain who it was pulling the strings before he laid the bait and drew them in. Luckily for DI Young the next City away game was a fixture at Nottingham Forest, his local team. Although that didn't leave the DI much time, he saw that as the perfect opportunity to make his move. He knew the hooligans at his local club well and they had a reputation the CBA couldn't ignore. What Young had to do was make the Londoners think that a hard core firm of Forest lads were planning to take their title away, and to do that he would use Billy Davis. He needed the druggie to forward false information to the contact known as 'London' that would lure the CBA to a prearranged meeting at a pub in one of the quiet back streets near to the train station. Inside the pub wouldn't be the local headcases the Londoners were expecting to fight with, but a firm made up entirely of police officers. The officers would need to play the game by calling the London hooligans on, and so the position of any filming equipment would have to be well planned in advance so as to avoid any accusations of 'incitement'. If he could track the firm and then film them attacking the pub he could throw the book at them. The recordings taken from Billy's phone would also add a conspiracy charge strong enough to send most of the CBA away for a good few years, and maybe even Billy as well, thus smashing the firm. More important to him though was the publicity and credibility the operation would most certainly receive from his superiors and in the media, as that would quickly send him shooting yet another step up the career ladder. To make sure 'London' telephoned Billy, DI Young would have to start the rumour about the so-called Forest firm before Saturday's game. The place to do that was The George and he knew just the way to go about it.

41

The George was even more crammed than usual. Everyone wanted to be associated with the lads who had done such a good job on Leeds the week before, and so the number of punters for this Saturday pre-match session was bolstered by the usual glory hunters. Mozzer didn't mind, he could see the eyes of those wishing they had the bottle follow his every move. Inside he felt they wanted to be him, top boy, and that made him walk with an extra spring in his step. He had given Camden and a few of his mates the task of scouting Kings Cross station for any Leeds firm, but with the time approaching midday he began to relax as, for them, time was running out. Sitting outside by the wooden tables were Officers Beck and Drummond. They didn't make the same mistakes as Lopes and Williams had done and were enjoying their second pint of the morning as well as joining in the banter with the lads around them. Beck got to his feet and headed for the toilet. Pushing his way carefully through the crowd he finally got to his destination and waited for one of the cubicles to empty. The door opened and Tony appeared, still tightening the belt on his jeans. He bumped into Beck.

'Sorry, mate.'

'That's all right. Mind out, though, I am busting.' Beck brushed past as Tony warned him of the imminent danger.

'I'd give that ten minutes if I were you, mate.'

The door shut as Tony walked off laughing to himself. The smell hit the back of Beck's nostrils. Immediately he blew the air back out.

'Jesus!' He quickly undid the button of his shirt pocket and pulled out the piece of A4 paper and some business cards. He unfolded the paper, removed the backing from the double-sided tape and stuck the mini-poster to the side wall. He pressed firmly, making sure it held the position then listened to make sure the toilet was empty. He unbolted the door, dropped some of the business cards and went to make a hasty exit. As he pulled the door open Doug was coming in the opposite direction. The Londoner fell forward, as his expected push to open the door was stolen away from him and he collided with Beck.

'Way. Sorry, geezer.' Beck just smiled and shot past the Londoner. He needed to get out quick before Doug spotted one of the cards. He pushed his way through out into the open air and back to Drummond.

'We're off. *Now.*' His colleague sensed the urgency in his voice, left his pint and quickly followed behind.

Back in the toilet Doug was enjoying his piss. He had noticed the cards on his way in but his bladder had told him to empty himself out before even thinking about doing anything else. Kelly entered the lavatory.

'Some dickhead's dropped his cards – look.' Doug nodded in their direction. 'Have a look an' see whose they are.'

Kelly bent down and picked one of the cards up from the floor. Doug noticed a surprised look cross his face that then turned to anger. Kelly bent down and took another card from the floor.

'Is this a fuckin' piss-take or what?'

'What? What's it say?'

Kelly grew more angry. He turned and kicked open the door of the cubicle hoping to find the enemy hiding away inside. His body shook with disappointment at the empty sight that greeted him. His eyes focused on the small poster stuck to the wall. He moved forward to study the words.

'*Fuckin' wankers.*' He ripped the paper from the wall and stormed out leaving Doug none the wiser.

'What is it, for fuck's sake?'

The door slammed behind Kelly, leaving Doug alone once more. He pulled up the fly on his strides then bent down to read a card for himself. As he straightened back up he too got the message. '*Cheeky bastards.*' He bent back down and gathered the rest of the cards. 'The lads are going to love this.'

Kelly pushed his way through to where Mozzer and Baggy were sitting. Danny, Stokey and Dean were following close behind.

'Take a fuckin' look at that.' Kelly rammed the poster in front of Mozzer. The shock made him jump and knock the table, nearly sending his pint flying. He grabbed for his glass.

'Fuckin' easy, you prat.'

Kelly took no notice. 'That's a fuckin' piss-take, that is.'

Mozzer snatched at the piece of paper while fixing a glare on Kelly. 'This better be bloody good, son.' He turned and smoothed the poster out on the table for all to see. The words stood out in big bold letters.

WHO THE FUCK ARE LEEDS ANYWAY?

THE C-B-A

CAN'T BATTER ANYONE

WATCH YOUR BACKS AT FOREST

BE SEEING YOU!

Baggy was first to speak. 'Where'd you find that?'

'In the fuckin' bog just now. And there's these.' He flicked the cards onto the table. 'The fucker who did this must have been in here this morning.'

Dean butted in. 'That's bang out of order. That's taking fuckin' liberties, that is.'

Baggy turned to Mozzer. 'He's right, Mozzer. We can't let that go.'

Kelly continued. 'We're up there next week, Mozzer. Some bastard's goin' to pay for coming on our patch and dropping this.'

Mozzer tried to calm the situation. 'Ease up, lads.'

Stokey was straight back in. 'Fuck ease up, Mozzer. That's out of order.'

The main man wasn't accustomed to coming under so much pressure from his troops but the lads were raging. He turned to Baggy for support but received none.

'They're right, Mozzer. We gotta go do it.'

For the first time Mozzer wished he had told Baggy about the connection between his contact and the police identity card taken from Lopes' jacket. This poster from the Forest lads made that three links with the city of Nottingham and now Mozzer was beginning to get a gut feeling that made him more than a little uneasy.

42

The white Transit turned into the side road and found itself a place to park. Another van pulled alongside and the drivers spoke through the open windows.

'Go find a space and we'll wait here.' The driver stretched his neck to look back down the road he had just driven up. Behind the van he could see the three motors that made up the rest of the convoy. 'I'll tell them to do the same, but hurry.' The van pulled off followed by the cars. The back doors sprung open allowing its contents to spill out. Ten lads, then three more, another two.

'Get the kit bags and the cool box over 'ere.' With the van empty and the back doors ajar, he opened the bag and began to lay the weapons out. Three baseball bats. Five half pool cues. There were darts, hammers, golf balls and short solid lengths of steel.

He addressed the impressed onlookers. 'I know you all have your own tools, but take what you need from here as back-up.' He moved aside as eager hands grabbed at the armoury. He placed the small red cool box on the pavement, took a quick look around and then removed the lid. He was greeted by a sight that made him nod his head with approval.

'Fucking beauties.' Inside the box were two laced petrol bombs and a CS gas canister. He replaced the lid as quickly as he had removed it. He looked up. Coming towards him were the passengers from the rest of the convoy, some 45 lads in total and every one tooled-up.

'Right, let's fuckin' do it once an' for all on these Cockney bastards.'

The firm turned and marched down the quiet, almost deserted, back street.

43

Beck and Drummond were now sitting back in the safety of the unmarked police car. DI Young was pleased with his officers' actions.

'Well done, Beck.'

The adrenalin was still pumping inside him. 'That was a bloody close call that was.' He laughed excitedly. From across the green they had a clear view of the pub. Some of the lads were enjoying the midday sun, but the majority of the firm were tucked up inside the bar before heading off to the match.

DI Young fixed his eyes on the front entrance. 'Did you recognise any of the faces?'

Drummond answered. 'Oh yes, sir, they're all in there. Plus another 100 at least, I'd say.'

'Good.' He turned to his stooges sitting on the back seat. 'You two, along with Lopes here, should keep well out of sight for the rest of the day. Keep observing, but keep a safe distance. We have plenty of other men around who can get in among them.' He turned his attention back to the pub. 'We very nearly have this little lot in the bag.'

Drummond suddenly shot forward in his seat and pointed across to the other side of the green.

'Who the hell is that little lot?' All the eyes fixed on the mini army quickly making their way across the turf towards the pub.

Lopes was taken aback. 'Fucking hell, this looks heavy.'

DI Young was on the radio in a shot.

'All units. All units. Observe a large gang crossing the Green heading in the direction of the target building. Stay in your positions. Film if possible but, I repeat, do not leave your position.'

Drummond went for his phone. 'We better get some local plod down here sharp.'

DI Young shot around and knocked the mobile out of his officer's hand before he could dial even one digit. 'Fuck the local plod. This is my operation, you hear? *Mine.*'

44

Charlie was enjoying another cool mouthful of the golden liquid when his eyes first caught sight of the mob heading towards him. At first it didn't register, and for a split second he watched as they came closer. Suddenly his mind smacked in as if he had just taken a solid right hook on the nose. At first the words were spoken as if only to himself, then he shouted at the top of his voice.

'What the fu . . . FUCKING HELL.'

The heads of those around him turned. The mob knew they had been sussed and broke into a jog. As the rush hit them they started to shout.

. . . LEEDS . . . LEEDS . . . LEEDS . . .

Now they were running, closing in on their target. More shouting. Louder. Aggressive.

. . . LEEDS . . . LEEDS . . . LEEDS . . .

Some of the Londoners stuck outside the pub ran, their bottle gone. Others grabbed for any glasses that lay around. The Yorkshire mob pulled up as they got to the opposite side of the road. They jostled, arms wide, waiting. They called the Londoners on.

. . . COME ON, YOU COCKNEY BASTARDS . . . COME ON . . .

Charlie charged through the pub doors.

'GET THE FUCK OUTSIDE NOW. WE'RE BEING FUCKIN' HIT.'

Those inside the bar rose as one and piled towards the door.

At the front of the Leeds firm, the Transit driver stepped forward. He took the lid from the cool box and removed one of the petrol bombs. As cool as could be he took his lighter and sparked up the rag that hung out of the top of the milk bottle. Then, taking two steps forward, he launched his weapon. The missile, with its warm glow trailing across the skyline, seemed to hang in the air for ages. All eyes followed its path until it finally came crashing down to earth. The glass shattered and the liquid spread itself across the concrete. A bang ripped through the air, followed by a whoosh as the petrol ignited. The yellow and orange flames spread themselves in every direction, sending the Londoners running for cover. The Yorkshireman lit up the second missile. Again he launched it forward, only this time his aim was much better as it came crashing down directly in front of the doors. The flames shot through the opening and into the pub, lighting the clothes of some of the punters trying to get out. Screams joined the smoke and flames in the hot air as panic set in.

For the Leeds firm the petrol bombs had served their purpose and cleared the way. They steamed forward, screaming out their hate-filled cries. Golf balls pelted the windows, sending glass flying onto those trapped inside. The Yorkshiremen had the front of the pub to themselves now as all the Londoners had scattered. Inside they could hear the shouts of those desperate to get out and take up the challenge. Once more the driver led the charge and headed towards one of the now-smashed windows. He took the green canister of CS gas, pulled the ring from the top and threw it into the mayhem taking place on the other side of the brickwork. He moved back to join the rest of his troops as they waited to pick off their prey.

Inside it was chaos. Mozzer could see the flames beating back his lads as they tried to escape. Glass showered his table as people ran in all directions, shouting, screaming. Over at the door he could see three lads he knew from south of the river, their clothes on fire.

'DEREK, GET THE FUCKIN' FIRE HOSE. QUICK.'

Stokey wrapped his jacket around one of the lads' legs, dampening the flames, as others searched for a way out.

Baggy was over by the door of the back room. He shouted to be heard over the noise.

'THIS WAY. OUT THE BACK, COME ON'

The regular lads followed, leaving the glory-hunters fighting the fire. Mozzer was over the bar like a shot as Derek appeared with the fire hose. As Mozzer disappeared through the escape route, the mist of the CS gas was spreading itself out. Clive was caught. His eyes began to sting. He covered his face and began to rub his eyes. Quickly he became short of breath, his eyes watering, stinging. His nose felt as if it were on fire as the retching smell hit the back of his nostrils. It became harder to breathe. He coughed, then began to choke. He rubbed harder, his skin beginning to burn. He needed to get out. Others were experiencing the same. Panicking. The air was filled with the sound of people's agony, their coughing, choking. Cries for help rang out. Derek turned the hose full blast on the flames, then hit the canister sending it spinning across the floor. Clive grabbed his chance. The flames were now a thing of the past. He badly needed fresh clean air in his lungs. He rushed through the door followed by Stokey. The other lads who had been trapped inside fought to get out, away from the choking mist. As they spilled onto the street many fell to the floor grasping at the air. Clive couldn't see, his eyes still burning. He tripped and stumbled forward, coming to rest on all fours.

'Someone help me, HELP ME.'

The only people waiting to greet them were the lads from Yorkshire.

The baseball bat came crashing down across his back, forcing what little air he had inside from his lungs. He crumpled on the floor. His attacker lifted the bat once more, only this time high above his head.

'Have this, you Cockney bastard.' It rushed through the air then smashed into Clive's shoulder. The crack rang louder than the chaos going on all around. Clive couldn't scream, his lungs empty. Inside the pain overtook all the other feelings he had. He felt his body shudder as a boot landed in his stomach, only now his body had begun to shut itself off and there was no more pain.

The Yorkshiremen took their pick as pool cues, hammers and coshes all hit their targets. Stokey battled against his streaming, stinging eyes, trying to stop wave after wave of punches. His arms flayed about in front of him in the vain hope of scoring the odd hit himself. He caught the flash of light as it flew through the air. At first he felt nothing. The attack stopped. He rubbed his cheek then continued to hit out at nothing but air. His eyes began to clear. His skin felt hot and he began to wobble on his feet. He felt his cheek once more. Again he rubbed at his stinging eyes. His hand felt sticky. He looked at it. Red. He began to see clearly for the first time, then his stomach began to feel nauseous and he wobbled once more. He spread his arms out, looking for trouble.

'Come on, you wankers.' He began to wobble as his attacker moved away from him. The Yorkshireman turned and was on his toes. Stokey's world went misty. He shook his head then fell back against the wall, bringing his hand up once more to rub his stinging cheek. As he rubbed, the fingers worked their way under the skin. They moved inside the flesh. His mind was picking up strange messages, messages it didn't understand. Sticky, wet, heat. He pulled his hand down and tried to focus on the image. All he could see was a crimson mass of blood. Deep red crimson. His blood. The fluid dripped from his fingers onto the floor. The sight shocked him to his senses. Once more he rubbed the cheek. This time his whole hand found its way inside the wound. His fingers moved and prodded their way forward as a strange feeling came over him, almost calm. They touched bone. He pressed, feeling for a clue, then he realised he was touching his teeth. A sweet, metallic taste filled his mouth and clogged his throat. He spat a deep red puddle onto the floor. He staggered, trying to figure out what was happening to him, then let out his cry.

'I've been cut, I'VE BEEN FUCKIN' OUT.' Stokey became hysterical, searching out for help, screaming at the top of his voice. He fell to the pavement and, once there, thankfully he blacked out.

Mozzer came steaming out of the back alley and onto the main road. The rest of the lads charged out behind him, screaming their anger. Cars were sent skidding to avoid collision, the drivers spinning their wheels in order to escape the chaos taking place. The Leeds firm hadn't expected a second wave of troops, they were still busy smashing the heads of the easy pickings spilling out from the main pub entrance. Clarkie waded in for all he was worth, bringing down one unprepared northerner and smashing his head hard into the tarmac. As the lad tried to gather himself Clarkie sent an empty beer bottle crashing down onto his head with a dull shuddering thud. The lad made one last effort at escape then lost consciousness. Clarkie moved forward as the Londoners began to drive the Leeds firm back across the road and onto the Green. Both groups tried to gather themselves, the Leeds lads particularly keen to avoid getting split up. Once more they came forward, their weapons ready to inflict as much damage as possible. The wind whistled past Baggy's face as the pool cue missed by the thickness of a coat of paint.

Pinhead fronted the lad. This northern bastard who had come to take the piss in his own back yard. Pinhead knew the risks. If he got hurt then fuck it, it was part of the game. Some you win some you lose but no way was he going to back off when he was at 'home'. The two of them fought out their own private battle of wits. Pinhead edged back then darted forward as if to attack, trying to draw his opponent on. The Yorkshireman held his baseball bat out, waving the end in front of Pinhead's face, just waiting to pounce.

The Londoner shot a look over the right shoulder of his attacker. 'NOW. DO THE FUCKER.' He darted forward at the same time. The Yorkshireman spun around expecting to be jumped from behind, swiping the weapon into thin air as he turned. The bluff had worked. Pinhead took his chance. He dived low and took away the feet of his target, bringing him

117

to the ground. He rammed his face into the hard mud as the bat went spinning from his grip. Pinhead grabbed at his hair, lifted his face, then sent it smashing once more into the scorched earth. His opponent struggled but it was all in vain. Smash after smash, the grit and mud working their way under the skin. Skin that was now red raw, weeping.

Suddenly the chaos was shattered as the sound of police sirens began to grow louder. At once the fighting stopped, people pulled away from each other and there was a short silence as if time stood still. The sirens grew louder, closer. Most of the Leeds lads still standing began to turn on their toes and head back across the Green. Some remained, still wanting more but not knowing quite what to do. Others wanted to pick up their wounded and get them away from the grabbing hands of the Metropolitan police.

Mozzer ran forward and picked up the baseball bat.

'Pinhead. Hold that cunt there.' The youngster did as ordered. Then Mozzer shouted at one of the Yorkshiremen still caught in no man's land.

'OI, FUCK FACE. THIS ONE'S FOR YOU.' He turned and walked towards Pinhead, who was still sitting on the back of his prey. Baggy came and stood by his side. Mozzer sounded in total control as once more he ordered Pinhead into action. 'Hold his head up.'

He lifted the face out of the dirt as Mozzer slowly brought the bat above his head. He then shot one last stare at the Yorkshireman left helpless, watching. The lad on the deck opened his eyes, unsure of where he was, a gesture that brought an insane grin to Mozzer's face. He swung the bat down with full force, the wood cutting the air before smashing into the jaw. The crack, the ripping of flesh. Pinhead's grip was useless against the full force of the blow as the head shot back like that of a rag doll being violently shaken by a child. The neck fell limp. Mozzer was spun around with the force of the movement. He came to a stop facing the on-looking

Yorkshireman. Mozzer leant forward resting on the upright weapon. His voice remained totally calm against the insane act of violence. Mozzer addressed the Leeds lad once more.

'COME ON. COME AND GET YOUR MATE.'

Pinhead got to his feet, his eyes fixed on the body lying beneath him. The sirens grew louder still, then the blue flashing lights came darting into view. The sight broke the stalemate. The Yorkshireman turned and was away. Mozzer was also shaken into action. 'Let's get the fuck out of here.'

Pinhead remained motionless looking down at the body on the floor. Mozzer grabbed his shoulder and tried to shake some life into him. 'PINHEAD, YOU WANKER, LET'S GO.' Pinhead slowly moved back from the body, his gaze still fixed. He took slow, unsure steps backwards. Mozzer shook him violently then slapped his face.

'Let's fucking go. COME ON.' The lad suddenly came to life. He turned and began to run. Mozzer and Baggy chased after him.

45

'Did you get it? Did you get it, Lopes?'

'I got some good stuff sir. Bloody excellent. We'll put this lot away for years with this. Years.'

DI Young couldn't hide the excitement in his voice.

'Excellent. Now let's get the hell out of here.' He turned the key and the engine fired. The radio went into overdrive as his officers requested their orders. The DI directed them to meet in a side street just half a mile from where the violence had taken place. Once there, he would reassess the situation.

46

Mozzer pulled up, gasping for breath.

'We need to get the lads back together fast.'

Pinhead wasn't listening. 'I think you killed him, Mozzer.'

He sounded as if somehow he couldn't believe what he was saying himself.

Mozzer turned on Baggy. 'I told you, you daft cunt. I fucking told you Leeds would be back.'

Baggy was not in the mood for a lecture. 'Yeah, yeah. I fucked up. Now drop it.'

Mozzer was furious, strutting, turning this way and that as he tried to find the next words. They came out as if he were mocking a child. 'Yeah, Leeds won't be back. Leeds are nothing.'

'I said drop it, Mozzer.' Baggy's word sounded threatening but Mozzer continued.

'You prat Baggy. Thanks to you we weren't fuckin' ready and they took the fuckin' piss.' He spun round, unable to look at his right-hand man. 'We got done on our patch. Done on our own fuckin' turf.' Mozzer aimed a kick into the side of the car parked by him. His anger reached new levels. 'I DON'T FUCKIN' BELIEVE IT.' The metal buckled under the force of the attack.

'CALM DOWN, YOU TWAT.' Baggy was still desperately trying to get more air in his lungs. 'Get on the blower and put the word out to meet at The Manor.' He bent forward, resting his hands on his knees. 'If we are going to get any kind of result out of this then we'll need as many hands as we can get.' He looked up at Mozzer who was now calming down, listening. 'I reckon we should head up Kings Cross after the match, do it there. What do ya think?'

'Fuck after the game. What's wrong with now?'

'Yeah, right, oh, Mozzer. We ain't going to stand a bleedin' chance unless we have the numbers. Look, Leeds have to go to Kings Cross for the train north, don't they? If we do it my way we stand a better chance of getting a result.'

'You sure?'

'If we don't get these cunts then we can make some other fucker pay.'

Mozzer acknowledged the plan then started dialling. Pinhead remained in a world of his own, still shocked.

'Mozzer, did you hear me? I think you killed that bloke.'

Mozzer continued trying to contact his lads and turned away. Baggy answered for him, directing his anger at Pinhead.

'And? So fuckin' what. Why are you so fuckin' bothered? If he had've got the chance it would have been you biting the bleedin' dust, wouldn't it, eh?'

There was silence. Mozzer finished his first call and began dialling his second. As he did, he tried to reassure Pinhead.

'He ain't dead, you tart. Don't worry. He'll just be sucking through a straw for a few weeks, that's all.'

The phone connected and once more he turned away. The information he received back through his earpiece suddenly made him sound concerned.

'You're joking . . . That bad? . . . Is someone on it?'

Baggy and Pinhead straightened, wanting to know more. They watched as Mozzer listened. His face changed again as the anger began to well up inside.

'What Clive . . ? Right. Well done, Dean, son. I'll see you down at The Manor, OK? Someone's gotta pay for that, big time.' He placed the phone back in his pocket.

Baggy fired the question.

'What's up? What's goin' on?'

'That was Dean. He's waiting for an ambulance to turn up. Stokey got cut, bad.' He focused on Pinhead. 'And when we left, Clive weren't moving either.' He spat the words out. 'Still feel sorry for that northerner bastard, Pinhead?'

The youngster moved forward. 'They cut Stokey?' His own words brought him back to reality. 'I'll flag us down a cab.' He ran out into the road and pulled over the first black taxi that came towards them.

47

Once more the stadium was heaving. Inspector Driver had again allowed his northern colleagues into his control room. On the screens DI Young watched as his targets moved among each other, agitated, planning. Driver had heard rumours about the morning's violence and wanted to know more.

'I hear there has been a spot of trouble down at Ealing earlier?'

'Yes, you could say that, Inspector.' DI Young continued to give away his knowledge without thinking as he studied the video panel. 'Your local headcases have been hard at it the last few weeks. This morning they came unstuck.'

'Really?'

Lopes butted in, so as to stop his superior giving away too much. 'Yes. It wasn't that bad, really. A few of this lot ran into some Leeds supporters and took a bit of a beating, that's all.'

DI Young realised his mistake and remained quiet.

'Serves the idiots right. Anyway, that's not my problem. As long as they don't step out of line in here then that's OK.'

DI Young focused his attention once more on the screens. In particular, he fixed his gaze on the lad constantly moving to and fro. The lad holding the mobile phone to his ear, the lad he knew to be Steven Morris.

Down in the seats Mozzer was busy. His anger at being turned over had set him off on a mission, a mission of total revenge. Dean had returned from the hospital and relayed the news to the rest of the CBA troops. The news spread quickly among the lads, whipping up a hate and anger that was almost visible. Clive had been kept in suffering from back and shoulder injuries, as well as concussion. And Stokey had needed 16 stitches in his cheek. The only saving grace, as far as the firm were concerned, was the news that one Leeds fan was in a bad way, suffering from head injuries and a broken jaw. Most of the other lads had received treatment for the CS gas without having to go to hospital and the pub only suffered superficial damage. But every one knew that Leeds had come down and scored a major result. If the CBA were going to save face then it would have to be done today. Mozzer never once focused on the football being played out in front of him. He didn't notice the breathtaking strike from 35 yards that sent City in 1–0 up at half-time, or the second goal ten minutes into the second half that made it 2–0. He had other things to think about, plans to make.

Mozzer watched the scoreboard, waiting. Then the signal came. The clock ticked over. Eighty minutes played. As one, the CBA rose to their feet and made to the exit. Over in other parts of the ground the same thing happened as groups of lads stood, then turned to leave. The rest of the spectators wondered at the spectacle. The stewards and police looked on bemused as 200, 500, 1,000 lads in various parts of the stadium made their way to the exits. The Newcastle fans began to taunt them.

. . . WE CAN SEE YOU SNEAKING OUT . . . WE CAN SEE YOU
SNEAKING OUT . . .

As the numbers grew the Geordies fell silent and they began to fear that they may be the target of the firm's desire.

The sight sent shockwaves through the police control room. DI Young turned to Inspector Driver.

'What the hell is going on here?'

Driver moved towards the screens. 'I don't know. This is not the normal behaviour.' He began to order his men into action, fearing an attack on the visiting Newcastle supporters. 'Get all units down at the away turnstiles. NOW. Dog Units. Mounted Units, everything. Immediately.' The radios crackled and panicking voices filled the airwaves.

DI Young turned to his host. 'I think we better leave you to it, Inspector.' Driver didn't hear. He was already pulling on his coat and heading out of the door. 'Lopes, let's go. I only hope some of our lads are with that lot, otherwise we're knackered.'

The firms piled out onto the main drag, coming together in one heaving mass. As all police units headed off to protect the Newcastle fans, the City lads were given a free run down towards the tube station. They moved as one, breaking into a slow run, buzzing. The local residents and shoppers hid in doorways to avoid confrontation, as the mass headed past them unaware of their existence. They steamed the barriers and shot down onto the platform. Their timing could not have been better. The train opened its doors and within seconds the platform was empty. The firm were away, leaving only a handful of bemused uniformed police officers behind. They changed tube lines just once as they closed in on Kings Cross station. The Underground train came to a halt and the doors spat out its contents. The journey had been quick. They moved as a pack up the stairs to the escalator, knocking people aside as they went, uncaring. Mozzer needed his troops above ground. Down in the tunnels it was easy for the police to trap you and tie you up in knots. He wanted to draw the Leeds fans up and out into the open areas where there would be more room for them to fight. They oozed out onto the Euston Road and into the daylight. Mozzer took his lads and crossed the road. The other firms spread themselves out, ready and waiting for battle to commence.

One long minute passed then the first police riot van came weaving through the traffic and screeched to a halt by the railings opposite. The back doors shot open and emptied its contents as another van-load of filth pulled up alongside. There was no way Mozzer was going to let the pigs stop him having his revenge. He ran to the small news kiosk and grabbed at the stall holder.

'You, out the fuckin' way.' He pushed the owner aside and opened the fridge, then grabbed at the cans. 'Baggy, Kelly, 'ere quick.' He threw the full cans of drink to them. 'Do the Old Bill.' They didn't need telling twice. Baggy and Kelly knew as well as anyone that the police loved dishing it out when the odds were in their favour. Now the boot was on the other foot and it was pay-back time. Mozzer appeared just as an officer armed with a camera came out the back of the van. Surrounding him was his protection squad, his snatch squad. Mozzer had seen them before many times. They loved to incite people. They loved photographing them for no reason and then searching them in the street for all the tourists to see.

Mozzer steamed forward. 'KILL THE FUCKIN' BILL.' He launched a can directly at the cameraman. The rest of the City Army followed. The sound of the cans hitting the vans was deafening. The driver tried to move off but his way was blocked by the weight of traffic around him. Camden pulled at the door. The driver had shit himself at the sight of the firm and locked himself inside. Danny joined Camden. He pulled the cosh from his pocket and held it up for the terrified driver to see. Inside the cabin was panic. Outside Danny was having the time of his life. The cosh shattered the side window and in a flash Camden had released the lock and dragged the frightened copper out. The boots drove into his ribs as he tried to crawl under the van to safety. Mozzer homed in on his target as the City firm overran the defenceless boys in blue. The cameraman's protection squad had deserted him. He turned to run but the crash barrier blocked his path. Mozzer sent a flying kick thumping into the small of his back. The blow sent the copper crashing against the barrier, the wind spurting from his lungs. The camera fell from his grip. He tried to get to his feet and climb the metal railing in order to make his escape but Mozzer was having none of it. He dragged the copper down, grabbed the camera from the floor and smashed it into the face of the policeman. Years of pent-up hate for the boys in blue fired the shot. A thought flicked into Mozzer's mind. The copper being beaten by his own weapon. Mozzer loved that, he smashed the tool once more into the pig's face and followed it up with a boot to the groin. He ripped the film from out of the back then aimed the Nikon at the officer's head. It smashed into his cheek then bounced away on the pavement.

''Ave that, you filth bastard.' The officer then disappeared under an avalanche of boots. Mozzer jumped the barrier and went looking for more.

Baggy and Kelly had gone straight for the other van. The officers had no time in which to kit themselves out in their riot gear and became buried under the sheer weight of the onslaught. Kelly hoisted the truncheon from an officer's belt and cracked it down onto his head. Two hands tugged at his shoulder as one of the officer's colleagues tried to drag him off and make an arrest but the action was pointless as more of the City Army piled forward. Kelly shook himself free and spun around, the truncheon hitting its target full in the face, crunching the gristle at the bridge of the policeman's nose. He fell backwards, made useless. More sirens began to fill the air but there was no way this firm were going to stop. Suddenly the cry went up. The first load of Leeds fans had arrived at the station. The firm steamed inside. The roar became deafening as they searched out their targets. Windows came crashing down in the shops as people ran for their lives. Many of the Leeds fans ran. They didn't want any trouble, they weren't the type. But some, as ever, stood their ground. Mozzer respected lads like these. These were the top boys, prepared to take a battering for the club they loved so much. Mozzer had been in their position many times himself and so had all his lads. That was the bond all hard-core hooligans had. Joe Public didn't understand that, how could they with their safe little lives? That was why these hooligans stood shoulder to shoulder when travelling away with the England team. They understood what it's like to fight, to win, to lose. Today, though, they were bitter enemies and the battle raged on.

The City lads came in from all entrances, picking off anyone who stood in their way. Mozzer stopped to take in the sight. Baggy, as ever, was at his side.

'This is the bollocks, son. The fuckin' bollocks.'

Over by the newsagents he could see Stanard and his lads in full swing. They had emptied one of the vans of all its riot gear and were using the shields to force back a small group of lads doing their best to fight back. Mozzer and Baggy moved off in their direction. As they went, Baggy began to prize open the spikes on the rings he was wearing. He had fucked up back at The George this morning. He had told Mozzer that Leeds were a thing of the past and been proved wrong. Due to him, Clive was sitting in a hospital bed and Stokey had been badly scarred for life. Both those lads would have loved this. They would have lived off the stories for years, instead they were missing out and so someone was going to suffer.

Baggy attacked from the side, his fist colliding hard with the unsuspecting lad's temple. The spikes of the ring bit hard. They ripped into the flesh as Baggy turned his fist in order to wound as much as possible. The scream drowned out all other sounds. Baggy fired again. This time the ring caught the eye, the spike popping the soft white oval. The lad fell to the floor, screaming with pain, with fear, with uncertainty. He grabbed at his face, the blood pouring through the gaps of his fingers as he scurried around on the floor like a wasp that had lost its sting. The screams meant nothing to Baggy. He kicked at the lad's hands, whipping them away from his face and revealing the red ribbons of torn skin.

'That's for Stokey, you bastard.' Then he left the lad alone.

Suddenly the station fell quieter. All the battles were won and the station was theirs. They were kings once more. The cry went up.

. . . CI . . . CIT . . . CITY, CITY . . . CI . . . CIT . . . CITY, CITY . . .

They scouted the area, searching out more targets, but there were none. Just hysterical women trying to protect their children and old people standing looking shocked, bemused, dazed. A calm came over the firm as they took in the scene, the buzz dying down inside them all for a few moments.

The first police appeared through the entrance on Pancras Road, then more through what remained of the front entrance. The City firm stood their ground and watched as more and more police appeared. The barking of the police dogs rang loud within the confines of the station, and out on the road Mozzer could see more and more blue flashing lights by the second. He turned to Stanard.

'They ain't goin' to lift anyone, there's too many of us. But I ain't hanging around here for them to block us in.'

Stanard nodded his head. 'What do'ya think, then?'

Baggy joined in. He nodded towards the far exit. 'We can get out onto York Way. That's the best bet.'

The three lads began the move and their troops followed. As quickly as they had entered the station they were gone, out into the main road. Once more they brought chaos to the traffic. The police moved quickly to block off the entrance. At least they now had control of the station and could get the Leeds fans on their trains and out of the city. The police drew a line three deep across the road, stopping the firm from re-entering the station. At the front were the dog-handlers, the nastiest bastards of the lot. Mozzer knew the filth were in no mood to fight. Some of their lads had already taken a beating and they couldn't afford to lose any more against a firm this large. And, anyway, they knew full well that they would have their pay-back some other day, and with added interest.

Once more the buzz began to rise among the lads. It was early yet, surely there was more fun to be had. From the back of the crowd a cheer went up and Mozzer heard the noise of stampeding feet. The lads at the back were running, desperately trying to avoid the flurry of bottles and glasses that was raining down on them. From out of a pub further up the road more Leeds fans had appeared, ready to take up the challenge. These lads were real hard-core. Lads banned from going to football but still prepared to travel in order to get their fix of violence. Some Leeds fans sent running from the station had headed straight to the pub, a favourite first stop for thirsty northerners arriving in the capital, and called their lads into action.

Mozzer spotted the bottle as it spun through the air but Stanard wasn't so quick. It crashed hard against his head and down he went. Mozzer could already see the blood seeping its way through his hair as he tried to stumble back up. He took his shoulders and pushed him back down.

'Stay down, Pete.'

Stanard wanted none of it. He scowled at his mate. 'Let me up, you cunt.' Hastily he got to his feet but the quickness of his movement was too much. His head went misty, blank, then he became void. Mozzer and Baggy dragged him onto the pavement and rested him up against the wall. The shower of glass stopped and the cheer went up. The retreating City firm seized their moment and steamed forward.

'Baggy, we'll have to leave him, come on.'

Baggy took one last look at the victim out cold before him. The words were more for his own benefit as Stanard couldn't hear a thing. 'You'll be all right, son. Don't worry.'

He got up and chased after Mozzer. Once again the police were caught on the wrong side of the action as the Leeds and City fans fought yet another pitched battle on the streets of the capital. As the City fans drove the northerners back they turned their attention on the pub. Dean led the attack. Mozzer watched as his lad fired a rubbish bin through the smoke-stained window and for a few anxious seconds there was stillness as the firm waited for some kind of response. It came like a bomb exploding. Back through the gaping hole

came a shower of bottles, pool balls and then a wooden chair
– a clear signal from the northerners inside that they were
prepared to defend their small patch of London no matter
how much the odds were stacked against them.

Everyone turned on the building as Londoners searched
desperately for weapons. The pool balls were quickly snapped
up by eager hands and fired back through the window.
Suddenly the doors flew open and the Leeds lads steamed out
and straight into whoever came first. The northerners were
outnumbered some ten to one but they came out all guns
blazing. Mozzer could only admire their bottle. The Leeds
lads fought like dogs taking out Londoner after Londoner,
heads down, arms and boots flying. They fought together, as
one, and for a brief moment had the City lads backing away.
They knew the game well and were looking for a weakness, an
escape route, but slowly they became caged in as the
Londoners moved forward. Thankfully for Mozzer, the
Londoners had far greater numbers. He wouldn't have been
able to take being turned over twice in one day.

The task was too big for the northerners and so they
turned and ran back inside the pub. Once they saw the retreat
the City lads piled forward. The doors slammed shut just as
the first wave of Londoners arrived. The sheer weight of their
impact sent the doors crashing down off their hinges and the
way in was open. The Leeds lads had jumped the bar and were
now using every glass, bottle and ashtray they could find as
weapons. Mozzer was one of the first in. He dived under the
nearest table just in time as a bottle of Bud smashed against
the wall beside him. He could see his target lined up, gripping
hard on a smashed bottle, ready and willing to scar some
Cockney wanker for life. Mozzer grabbed the legs of the table
and, using it as a shield, he steamed forward, screaming out
his aggression and leading the charge. Others followed. The
Leeds lads were helpless against his barrier. Mozzer couldn't
see his way forward and crashed into the bar. The force of the

impact sent him rolling backwards. Out of the corner of his eye he could see the lad aim the bottle at his face. As quick as he could he brought his arm up to deflect the weapon but his defence came too late as it cracked against his temple. The thud turned the lights out on his world. All he could sense was the hateful cries that filled the room. Then searing pain shot through him. Hot agony. He let out a cry and rolled over, looking for a space to bring himself back to life. The room suddenly came back into focus.

The northerner was over the bar and bearing down on Mozzer like a rabid dog. He kicked and then fell on his prey, ramming both fists hard into his head, punching relentlessly. Dean smacked the chair full across the lad's face, the legs cracking, splintering with the force of the blow. The northerner's last punch caught nothing but fresh air as he fell back away from the main man of the CBA. Mozzer crawled away, still trying to bring himself back together as Dean finished the job by bringing what was left of the seat crashing down onto his enemy's head. He turned back to Mozzer who was now on all fours looking at the ground and shaking his head.

'Mozzer, we gotta get out quick.' He bent down, placed his arms around Mozzer's waist and lifted him to his feet. Suddenly Mozzer came back to life. All around him lay glass, broken wood and blood, his blood. He spotted the lad who had attacked him and the anger rose like a volcano.

'YOU BASTARD.' He searched out a broken bottle and grabbed at it. The lad on the floor had given up, the lights long gone out on his afternoon.

Dean shot a look towards the doorway. 'Mozzer, come on.' Dean's request went unheard. Mozzer walked over and straddled the lad who had just battered him. He pinned his arms out with his knees and clutched the chin firmly in his left hand. He rocked the face from side to side, searching out the right place just as an artist would, faced with an empty canvas. Mozzer picked his spot. The hate still burning in his words.

'You come down on my patch, arsehole.' The razor-sharp edge of the brown glass bottle drew the first line in the flesh of his forehead, then another. The blood began to run as the two lines joined and began to fold themselves outwards. Another straight line brought more of the crimson liquid flowing. Mozzer felt the warm blood touch his hand as the glass ripped through the tough skin. This time the cut went deeper and the wound began to gape open, a deep rich red hole. He began to hurry, the thought of someone else's blood on his skin now beginning to turn his stomach. Three more cuts and the job was done. He got to his feet and tossed the broken bottle aside. He stood next to Dean as the pair looked down at his masterpiece.

'There we go. Something for him to remember the day by.'

The blood ran over the northerner's face like water from a slow tap but Dean could just about make out the initials Mozzer had carved. They spelt out 'CBA'.

'Let's get the fuck out of here, Mozzer.' The two then turned and ran for the exit, leaving the pub battleground behind.

Once more the firm mobbed-up in the street. The police had kept a safe distance, knowing that there would be plenty of bodies to pick up and arrest once the main group had decided to move off. Slowly the City lads began to drift further north up York Way, allowing police to take control of the pub and get the ambulances in. Eventually the lads from the other firms began to drift off down the side streets and away, the buzz now at a low after all the excitement.

Baggy came over to where Mozzer and Dean were waiting. 'What now?'

'Better do the off. I need a drink.' Mozzer sounded tired, the wound on the side of his head now becoming the topic of Dean's conversation.

'I think you better get yourself cleaned up first.'

'Fuck me. What happened?' Baggy's question was pointless and Mozzer shot him an idiot's stare.

'Dean's right, I better get myself sorted. We ain't going to get any more action here. It's probably best that everyone goes their own way for a few hours to let the heat die down. We can all hook up later down the west end or something.'

'Fair shout. Wendy's away at the outlaws so we'll go back to my place, clean you up and make all the calls from there. I'll tell the lads.'

Mozzer agreed. They had done all they could to try and gain back some respect but deep down he knew that overall the lads from Leeds had really won the day.

48

At last DI Young's radio sparked into life. On the other end of the airwaves he could hear Detective Beck. Young was none too happy at being kept in the dark for so long.

'Where the hell have you been?'

'Sorry, sir, but there was no way we could contact you without getting our heads split open. You wouldn't believe what we have seen up here. It was total madness.' He filled his superior in on all the details and was then ordered to catch the first train back to Nottingham. DI Young shut the handset down.

'OK, Lopes, let's get back home and have a look at what we have in the way of video evidence. I'll just make one quick call before we set off.'

He pulled the notebook from his jacket, flicked the pages and then took up his mobile. The fingers on his right hand worked the numbers as the left hand clumsily held the little black book open. Two rings then the other end of the line answered.

'Hello.'

'Billy Davis?'

Billy immediately recognised the Detective Inspector's voice and couldn't hide his disinterest. 'Yes.'

'Billy, it's DI Young here.' There was a short silence. The policeman continued. 'Billy, have you had any contact with "our man London" today?'

Billy didn't like the term 'our man' one bit. Mozzer wasn't his man, he was his own man and no one else's. His answer was short and sharp.

'No.'

'That's good, Billy, good.' DI Young was relieved that he hadn't missed the chance to trap his prey. 'Right, I need to have a chat with you as soon as possible. I'd like to do that tomorrow, Billy. Is that OK?'

'Well, I suppose it'll have to be, won't it?'

The DI ignored Billy's unhelpful nature.

'I'll come to you at 10 o'clock in the morning, Billy. If you receive a call from the contact before then you must make sure he calls you back on Monday. Is that clear?'

Billy continued with his arrogance. 'I'll do my best.'

This time the DI bit back. 'Yes, Billy, you will.'

Billy didn't like the answer and by now he had had enough conversation with plod for one night. 'Is that it?'

'Yes. Until tomorrow.' This time DI Young hung up on Billy, knowing full well that that would leave his grass on edge.

49

Mozzer woke the next morning on the settee in Baggy's front room. As he sat up his head banged violently and he groaned out loud. At first he thought it was down to the beer, whisky and wine that he, Baggy and Dean had knocked back in celebration of the previous day's events. Then he rubbed his head and felt the lump by his temple. The pain forced him to fall back down. Baggy came in wearing nothing but a pair of boxer shorts.

'Fuckin' cheers, Baggy.'

The host placed a cup of hot sweet tea down on the table for Mozzer to drink. 'What?'

'I feel rough enough as it is without having to look at your sweaty bod first thing in the morning.'

Baggy turned around and pulled the back of his boxers down revealing the crack of his arse. 'You love it.' He tried to ram the exposed cheeks into Mozzer's face but they were quickly pushed away.

'Piss off.'

Baggy pulled up his shorts and began to laugh at his friend. 'Oh hang on.' He then dropped his shorts to let out a long booming beer fart. 'Yessss!' He punched the air with delight. ''Ave a tug on that, my old son.'

Although he had seen it a hundred times before Mozzer couldn't help but laugh. He sat up and took hold of his drink. 'You dirty bastard. Where's Dean?'

'He's having a shower. He looked rougher than you do.' He paused for a while. 'How's your head feeling?'

'It bloody hurts. Fuck that northern twat.'

'Dean told me what you did, carving the CBA in his forehead.' Baggy winced. 'Bloody hell, Mozzer, that was a bit strong.'

Mozzer showed no remorse. 'It'll give him something to look at every morning, won't it?' He rubbed his own wound. 'I may well be looking at this for the rest of my days.'

Baggy just raised his eyebrows and shrugged his shoulders. 'You want something to eat?'

'What you got?'

'You can have the full monty fry up if you want.'

Mozzer's stomach sent a quick message to his brain and he shook his head. 'No, don't think so. Toast would be good.'

'Consider it sorted.' Baggy got to his feet and walked off to the kitchen. He shouted out as he went. 'The papers are on the table if you want 'em.'

Mozzer perked up a little more. 'Is there anything about the trouble?'

'Is there bollocks. They give the team a good write-up though.'

Mozzer took the paper, sat back and started to check on yesterday's results. Dean entered the room.

'All right, Mozzer, how you feeling?'

'Fine.' He went to get to his feet. 'Look, Dean, I know I must have said this a hundred times last night, but I owe you one big time for yesterday.'

Dean cut in. 'Sit down, you ponce.'

'No, I mean it. I could have been out the race if it hadn't of been for you. It won't be forgotten. I am serious.'

Dean loved the attention and started to bait the main man. 'Oh don't get me wrong, Mozzer, I won't let you forget it. You owe me, all right.' He walked through and joined Baggy in the kitchen.

Mozzer turned his attention back to the paper.

Baggy's voice broke the silence. 'Doug left a message on the answer phone. It's a good job we stayed here last night, he reckoned the Old Bill were nicking everyone and anyone down the west end. Wankers.'

Mozzer took in what Baggy had said but sounded uninterested.

'Is that right?' He focused on the fixture list for next Saturday. Forest *v* City. For the first time he remembered the business cards and poster that Kelly had found in the toilet at The George. Baggy and Dean came back into the room and the smell of hot toast filled the air. As the smell worked up Mozzer's nostrils his stomach at last became human again. They sat in silence for a few moments as they satisfied their hunger. Mozzer hunted out his jeans and reached inside the back pocket. He unfolded the piece of paper and laid it out on the table before drawing it to the attention of the others.

'What we gonna do about this, then?'

Baggy took the question. 'Fuck. I forgot about that.' He read the words printed in thick black letters while he downed the remains of his tea. 'Well, we have to 'ave it, don't we? I mean, we can't let that go.'

Mozzer threw the same question to Dean. 'What do you reckon?'

''E's right, Mozzer. That was a fucking ponce's thing to do, dropping this in the pub and then fucking off. Wanker's trick, that.'

'I don't know. I've just got a feeling about it. Something ain't right.'

Baggy got to his feet.

'Well, after yesterday I ain't taking the responsibility for anything. I mean, I got it all tits up there, didn't I? If you say go, Mozzer, we go. If you say no, fair enough. It's your shout!'

Dean stared at Mozzer, waiting for some kind of reaction, then turned the conversation to the previous day's events.

'You gotta hand it to Leeds, they came and did the job on The George, fair play.'

Mozzer's mind also switched. He too was just as impressed. 'That was a top hit, I won't deny them that. I'll give Sheffield a call and tell him to pass on our respect.' He picked up the poster and re-read the words for the hundredth time. 'Well, after yesterday I suppose we have to put in a show. Let us hope Forest are just as game.' He tucked the piece of paper back in his jeans and took another slice of toast from the plate. He gazed into his empty cup and then up at Baggy.

'More tea, vicar!' Baggy headed back into the kitchen.

50

Yet again Billy Davis found himself sharing his table with the two policemen and once more DI Young was busy holding court.

'Billy, as I am sure you already know, City are playing at Forest next Saturday, yes?' Billy nodded. 'Right. That will mean that the lads from the CBA should be paying us a visit and I need you to ensure that this is indeed the case.'

The DI paused to give Billy a moment to reply. But the Londoner just took a fresh cigarette from his packet and sparked up once more without saying a word. DI Young took a piece of paper from his briefcase, laid it on the table and turned it around so that the lettering was the right way up for Billy to read.

'When "London" calls, and I am certain he will, this is the information I need you to pass him. You need to tell him that there is a firm of Forest lads planning a major hit on the CBA. They are not planning to hit with the rest of the Forest firm. Their plans are being kept very quiet, as they know they can only rely on having their top boys if they are to defeat the CBA. You understand, Billy?'

'Yes.' Billy's answer was sharp. He didn't like to be made out as an idiot by anyone, let alone a copper. He also didn't like hearing the lies he had to pass on to Mozzer. 'I understand. I can read it here, can't I?' His index finger stabbed at the paper, pushing it a little further away. DI Young edged the paper back and then continued to ram the message home.

'I want you to tell him that the Forest firm will be waiting in the White Lion pub on Sheriffs Way for the CBA to arrive. They will have spotters at the train station and out on the main route in from junction 24 of the M1. You must tell him that the Forest lads will be heavily tooled-up and are intending to do some really serious damage. That, Billy, is very important, you hear?'

Billy had heard enough and tried to gain back control of the situation. 'Look, just tell me what you have lined up for them.'

Detective Lopes snapped in. 'That's got sod all to do with you, Davis, you just do as you're told.'

Billy slouched back in his chair and shook his head at Lopes. The two fixed eyes but Billy's question was aimed at DI Young. 'Do you have to bring this monkey with you every time you visit my flat?'

Young tried to break their stare.

'Cut it out, gentlemen, please.'

Billy continued. 'Look, if I know what's going on then I can talk to him as if it's real and not being read from some scrap of paper, can't I?' He looked back at Young, trying to gain favour. 'I am trying to help.'

'Billy, all you need to do is get them to the White Lion pub and let him know these lads are serious. We take care of the rest.' A smile came across the DI's lips. 'If you do that then we can put an end to our "visits" and I can put my "monkey" here back in his cage.'

Lopes quickly turned his stare away from Billy and towards his superior. Billy began to laugh.

'Sounds a fair deal to me.' Then he took up the piece of paper, folded it in four, and tucked it into his back pocket.

As the two policemen walked down the path towards their car, Lopes spoke for the first time. 'If you don't mind me saying, sir, that was well out of order, you making me look a fool in front Davis like that.'

'For God's sake, Alan, grow up. Anyway you'll have the last laugh come Saturday night.' He walked around the car to the driver's side and placed the key in the lock. 'I tell you what. Once it's all over I'll give you half an hour in the cells on your own with him, how's that sound?'

'Yeah. In my bloody dreams.'

51

Mozzer had decided that it was best to throw a sicky and had taken the day off. The cut on the side of his head had now swollen to its maximum and the bruise was beginning to shine through. He felt that this was not the best impression to give his underlings or his clients but he still rose early. After a shower, shave and shit, Mozzer prepared himself some breakfast. He couldn't help but keep looking at the Forest warning poster that was now pinned up on his notice board. His mind was still working overtime on trying to figure things out.

> *. . . Fucking arse wipes . . . Who the fuck are Forest anyway? . . .*

The bang of the door made him jump. He pulled the belt tighter on his dressing gown and made for the hallway. The door knocker banged once more, the noise making him angry.

'Hang on, for fuck's sake. Give us a bloody chance.'

In a defiant gesture to make the person wait a little longer, he bent down to pick up his mail before opening the door. Pinhead was standing before him, his face lit up by the biggest smile Mozzer had ever seen. In his hand Pinhead was holding a copy of the *Daily News*, waving the paper in the air as if to tease Mozzer.

'What the hell's wrong with you?'

'Sorry, Mozzer, but I had to show you this. I rang work and they told me you were off so I came straight round. You ain't going to believe it.' Pinhead opened the tabloid and pointed to the article covering the entire area of page 7. Mozzer smoothed the paper and read the headline.

A RETURN TO THE DARK OLD DAYS AS FOOTBALL FIRMS CLASH ON THE STREETS OF THE CAPITAL LEAVING NINETEEN IN HOSPITAL.

Pinhead continued as Mozzer's eyes flicked across the words.

'We made the fuckin' papers big style, Mozzer. That will send a message to every other firm in London as well as all those northern ponces. It even mentions the CBA. It's fuckin' great.'

Mozzer tried to divert Pinhead's attention so as to give himself time to read the small black newsprint. 'Put the kettle on, will ya? And make it a strong one.' Mozzer began to laugh as the information filled his mind. 'What a load of bollocks. Have you read this? Listen. "If it hadn't been for the excellent display of police tactics, and their prior intelligence network, then the incident could have escalated into a full-scale riot." They got fuckin' battered.'

'It's a joke, ain't it? I was cracking up on the way over. Thing is, Mozzer, our reputation will rocket after that.'

'Yeah, trouble is, so too will the attention we get from the Old Bill. And if we want to get it on with Forest next week then we'll have to make sure the pigs are following some other little firm rather than us, won't we?'

As Mozzer read more of the article a cold chill worked its way down his spine. The paper reported that one lad was on a life-support machine after suffering serious head injuries during a pitched battle in west London. Inside, Mozzer knew that lad was the Leeds fan he had smacked with the baseball bat. As the image of the lad's face looking up at him shot into his mind Mozzer began to feel sick. He made his excuses to Pinhead before leaving the room.

'I better get dressed.' Mozzer headed off into the bedroom, sat himself down on the edge of his bed and began to chew at his thumb nail. His mind began to play tricks with him.

> . . . *What if the lad dies? . . . We're not meant to kill each other, for Christ's sake . . . There was no need to go that far . . . Don't worry. He'll be OK . . . He would have done the same . . . He was up for it, that's why he was down here . . . Please God, don't let him die. . .*

He rose to his feet, pulled on his clothes and headed back

out into the kitchen where Pinhead was once more pawing over the article.

'I am going to get this framed and hang it on the bog wall as a memento. It's bloody great that is.'

Mozzer's mind was still on the lad lying in that hospital bed but somehow he still managed to raise a laugh. 'Yeah, nice one, Pinhead. Nice one.'

'Let's hope for the same again next week, eh?'

Mozzer became confused. 'What?'

'Forest. Next Saturday.' Pinhead pointed to the poster on the notice board but Mozzer's reply was less than convincing.

'Oh yeah, right. That'll be sweet, that will.'

52

Billy took little time in packing away what he wanted from his spare room. Lopes had virtually shut his drug business down following his wrecking spree and so there was not really much left of any use to him. He took the screwdriver from the tool box and began to work on the screws at the back of his small chest of drawers. Once all eight screws had been removed he used the tip of the tool to prize the wooden panel away, revealing the hiding place. As ever, his face lit up as his eyes set themselves on the wonderful sight. His hands quickened as they grabbed at the money. Wad after wad of used notes came from the stash hole. Tenners, twenties, all used, all kosher. When Billy received the tip-off about the drug raid, not only did he remove his weed plantation but his money bank as well. He hadn't told anyone what lay in the bottom of the chest of drawers as money often turned people into thieves, and Billy couldn't risk losing his nest egg and life savings all in one go.

Billy had locked the door behind himself so that he was trapped in a world of his own. The curtains had also been tightly drawn to stop any prying eyes from catching an insight into his private little bank vault. He went through the ritual of counting the money and, to his delight, the final figure reached the total he had expected – £22,680. Billy laughed to himself as he remembered Lopes playing the hard man whilst he smashed up every other item of the furniture in the room apart from the one Billy had just dismantled himself. If only the 'monkey' had known just how close he had been to discovering this little nest egg for himself. After all, if Lopes had found the money Billy wouldn't have had a leg to stand on. He could hardly have run to the police, could he? And so there would have been nothing stopping Lopes and his side-kick, Detective Beck, from placing the cash straight into their own pockets.

Billy sat surrounded by his money and thought for a while. He knew that if he wanted to he could end all this over just one phone call. He thought of Davy Philips, his dead best friend and the old leader of the CBA. He thought of Mozzer, DI Young, and then of that bastard Lopes. Boy, did he have a score to settle with that monkey Lopes. First he counted out £1,500 then carefully placed the rest of the cash back into the darkness of its hiding place. Billy then refitted the wooden panel and edged the chest firmly back against the wall. As he left the room for the kitchen the telephone began to ring. Billy stopped short and checked his watch. It was 1.15 p.m. He heard the click of the tape machine as it went to work. On all the previous occasions the telephone had rung at this time he had hoped that the voice on the other end of the line would be anyone's but Mozzer's. But for Billy this time things were different. He knew that if anyone was going to be playing games this Saturday then it would be him.

53

Mozzer really didn't fancy the off with the Forest lads as there were too many iffy questions tapping away at his brain for his liking. Unfortunately, the rest of the lads were well up for it. They were gagging for more action following on from the violence of the previous two weekends. The poster in the pub toilet had set them right off and the newspaper article would fire them up even more. Mozzer knew they wouldn't let him off lightly if he failed to come up with the goods on this occasion. Curiosity had also got the better of him and so once again he had dialled the number of his contact. The telephone rang six times before the connection was made.

'Hello.'

'Hello. London here.'

'Ah, excellent. I was hoping you would ring.' The tone of the contact's voice took Mozzer by surprise. He had never sounded that enthusiastic before on hearing his voice and it made Mozzer pay even greater attention.

'Oh yeah? Why's that then?'

'I have some very interesting information for you about the Forest boys next week.'

Mozzer wanted more. 'I've heard rumours meself, but go on.'

'There is a firm lining you up for next week. It's away from the main firm, a real hard core.'

'How many?'

'Forty, fifty maybe. Nasty bastards out to make a serious name for themselves, starting with one big hit. A hit on the CBA.' The lies came easy to Billy. It didn't matter to him that he was setting up a man he felt he knew as a friend. Inside the feeling was good, a feeling of total control.

'They will be tooled-up in a big way,' he continued. The other end of the line remained quiet as Mozzer digested the information. 'Are you still there?'

Mozzer finally answered. 'Yes, I am still here.' Usually he didn't ask too many questions during these calls and once again alarm bells were ringing in his head. 'How did you get all this?'

The question threw Billy and his answer became

aggressive. 'What's the problem, London? 'Ave I ever told you shit before?'

Mozzer was jolted by the tone of the reply. 'Well, no.'

'Fuckin' right, no. Now if you don't want to listen, put the fuckin' phone down.'

Mozzer became defensive, apologetic. 'No, sorry. Please carry on.'

Billy began to calm down and tried to convince Mozzer that his information was straight. 'Look, this is my patch. I know these people, right? They don't know I am talking to you, of course, but I know them. Trust me.' Billy paused for a few seconds, then: 'Davy Philips did.'

Those last three words brought Mozzer round. Davy Philips had been a good friend to him when he was younger, and the mention of his name restored total trust in the contact Davy had supplied him with some three years back. For Billy, the feelings were different. For the first time he felt on edge. He was using the name of his dead best friend to place Mozzer in danger. Billy began to wonder if his plans would work or how he would feel if everything went wrong. Mozzer broke the short silence.

'OK. Do you have anything else to tell me?

'Yes. They will be mobbing-up in the White Lion pub on Sheriffs Way. They'll have spotters out all over the place as well, so if you want to hit them you'll have to be clever about it.'

'Right, got it.'

Once again there was a short silence before Billy passed on his final few words. 'Remember this lot are, well, naughty. They will be well tooled-up, so watch yourself. And finally, don't use the station.'

'Why not?'

'The Old Bill are cunts up here. They'll be all over that place.'

'OK, then. Nice one. Look, we'll do this one for Davy, all right?'

Billy let out a short laugh. 'Yeah, why not, he'd have liked that. Speak to you soon, and have a good one, won't ya!' He finished the call with a small word of concern. 'London, be lucky.' The line went dead and the tape recorder clicked once more, only this time it ground to a halt.

54

Mozzer placed the mobile down on the table and began to rub his face with both hands. The contact had never come across like that before. The manner in which he spoke was different. The certainty of the information. His aggressive nature and the length of the call. Everything was different. Mozzer sat himself down, then got to his feet. He switched the television on. The sight and sound of Puff Daddy spouting bullshit yet again on MTV was the last thing he needed, and so the screen quickly became blank again.

'Wanker. Bullshit music.'

His mind was scrambled.

> *. . . The contact was right, he had never let him down before . . . Davy trusted him, surely that was good enough . . . It always had been in the past, so fuck it . . . don't worry too much . . .*

He grabbed his keys from the table and made his way down to the Underground station.

> *. . . Fuck it. If I am going to Nottingham I better look the part . . .*

He entered the building, bought himself a Travelcard and headed off up the west end.

55

Once again the operations room was crammed as DI Young led the first briefing of the week. Billy had telephoned Young immediately to inform him that 'London' had made contact and so Detective Hunt had been dispatched to retrieve the taped conversation. The officers sat and listened in silence as Billy fed the false information. The only noise coming when Billy referred to the local constabulary as 'cunts'. Not surprisingly, it was only Detective Alan Lopes who failed to see the funny side of Billy's little dig.

'As you just heard, gentlemen, Mr Davis did an excellent job for us. That, along with the dropping-off of the poster and business cards at their local drinking hole last week, should ensure that we have a busy time this coming Saturday.' Once more he went over the details of the planned set-up with his men before watching the video footage shot by Lopes of the fighting at The George pub for the first time.

'Now I want you to watch carefully. What we need to do here is pick out the faces of the ringleaders. We need to know which of these men are likely to cause us the most problems.' He took a batch of photographs in his hand and held them up. 'You all have copies of these pictures, I take it?' A muttering rippled its way across the room. 'I want names put to faces. Is that clear? I want the names of the really violent ones, the ones who will cause most damage given half the chance.' DI Young ordered Detective Drummond to pull down the blinds, then set the video to play.

Slowly they worked through the footage. The level of the violence shocked many of the officers who were in the room for the first time. The organisation shown by the firm from Leeds was something they had never expected to see. Previously they had thought that the football hooligans were nothing more than chancers, out for a punch-up with whoever they could find – just gangs of brain-dead Neanderthals in football shirts, pissed-up mouthy bastards. Now they knew different. What they were viewing had taken serious planning. It was premeditated, meticulous and very violent. The thought that they could well be in the firing line come Saturday was beginning to have a few rings twitching.

DI Young stopped the video just as Mozzer and the lads were first seen coming out from the side alley.

'Right, gentlemen. Forget all you have just seen. It is here where we take an interest.' He used a pointer to pick out the lads of the CBA. 'These are the men we shall be dealing with next week.'

One by one he pointed at the faces on the screen. Slowly he motioned the images forward as his men matched the faces on the screen with the pictures in their hands. Then they matched the names to faces. Slowly the images moved on. The violence continued. Grown men in their 20s, 30s, some even in their 40s, violently kicking and punching away at each other in what DI Young and his colleagues believed to be their misguided support of a football team. Detectives Lopes and Beck loved it. They were busy making out they couldn't wait to get at the 'Cockney wankers'. Busy playing the hard men, geeing up their colleagues. Most played the game but inside others were not feeling so brave. Young stopped the film and grabbed everyone's attention.

'Now, gentlemen. Just in case anyone in here still thinks that next week will be a pushover,' he paused and threw Lopes and Beck a knowing look, 'then let me draw your attention to this.' He pointed to a group of three lads standing above the body of a young man lying on the ground. 'This young man here holding the baseball bat. I want you all to watch what happens over the next few seconds. This will prove to you just how far these people are prepared to go.' He turned to face the screen and flicked the video machine on to slow motion. The room fell silent as the man with the baseball bat brought it down across the face of the lad on the floor. Every officer in the room winced, letting forward a groan of pain. DI Young stopped the video and turned back to his men.

'That, gentlemen, is what we are up against. And if you are not careful next Saturday then it could be you on the end of that baseball bat. Understand?'

Drummond raised his hand. 'Sir, do we know who that man is?'

'As you can see, Drummond, we do not get a good enough look at that particular lad's face. Not good enough to hold up in court any way. However, I personally believe that man is one Steven Morris, otherwise known as Mozzer. He is the man I believe to be the leader of this firm. Everyone make a note of that name.' He paused for a moment allowing everyone to focus their attention on him. 'He is the man I want to trap most of all.'

DI Young finished his briefing and then made his excuses and left the room, leaving Lopes to take control. The officers viewed the footage. Then again, and again. Each time the actions of the lad with the baseball bat brought the same painful groans.

56

Billy made his way from the bedroom to the kitchen and put the kettle on. As usual he had rolled his early morning spliff the night before and was already tooting happily away. He opened the back door and went out into the glorious daylight for the first time. The sun, even at this early time of day, warmed his skin as the cool fresh air joined the sweet-tasting smoke in his lungs. He checked his motorbike while the water heated itself in the kettle. He opened the top box, took out the map book and went back inside to make his drink. Billy felt he needed a few days by the seaside and the weather couldn't have been better. He studied the map carefully, thinking to himself.

*. . .Yarmouth? No, might bump into some old faces . . .
Aberystwyth? Too many Welsh . . . Brighton? Definitely
not . . . Weston-Super-Mare? Never been there . . .* His
mind paused for a moment . . . *In fact, don't know
anyone who has . . . Actually, that ain't such a bad idea
. . .*

Suddenly he became excited, just as a school child would
during the summer holidays. He quickly gulped down his
coffee then reached for the packet of Cornflakes that was
sitting innocently on the sideboard. He buried his hand deep
inside and removed the £1,500 he had counted out the day
before from its new hiding place. As ever, he counted the
money first then went to the cupboard in the hall and took
out his riding leathers and crash helmet. Billy stuffed the wad
of money into his jacket pockets as he made his way back
outside and climbed across his GPZ. He didn't bother to pack
any other clothes as he knew he would be back tomorrow. All
he needed were his plans, and they were firmly tucked away
in his mind.

57

Mozzer added a hint of sickness to his best telephone voice.
'Shirley. It's Steven.'

'Hello, love. How you feeling today?'

'Oh a lot better, thanks, but my tummy's still a bit dodgy,
you know. Look, I've got lots of paperwork to catch up on, so
I think I'll stay at home again today and battle my way
through that. OK?'

'Oh yes, of course, you look after yourself. If anything
really urgent crops up I'll give you a bell. Otherwise I'll hold
all your calls until tomorrow. Don't worry.'

'Shirley, you're an angel.' Whilst on the line Mozzer
couldn't resist the temptation of doing even the smallest slice

of business. 'Oh, by the way. Give Colin a bell, will you? Tell him to get himself down to Aquaprint in Beckenham. I was with a guy on Thursday and they want to place an order, pronto.' Mozzer could hear her busily scribbling away.

'Aquaprint, Beckenham. Lovely. OK, Steven, I'll call him right away.'

'Tell him I expect to see the business done and on his work report by Friday. Cheers, then, Shirley. See you tomorrow.'

As soon as the line went dead Mozzer dialled a fresh number. He checked his watch. 8.47 a.m. Just two rings and the familiar voice answered at the other end.

'Choice Despatch, how can I help you?'

'You can help me by tugging your strides down, stickin' a broom up your arse and sweeping my front room.'

Baggy started laughing. 'Who the fuck's that?'

'It's Mozzer, you prat. Who'd you think it was?'

'I don't know, do I? It could have been anyone.'

'What, you got a lot a mates like that, have ya?'

'You'd be surprised what I get up to in the privacy of me own home, Mozzer. What the fuck do you want anyway?'

'I wondered if you fancied a day out?'

'What, you off work?'

'Throwing a sicky.'

'Oh, fair enough. Where d'ya want to go?'

'Nottingham.'

Baggy had hoped for somewhere a little more exciting. 'Nottingham? What for?'

'I had words with me contact yesterday. He told me a bit about this Forest firm and the pub they use. I reckon it's worth checking out.'

Baggy began to flick through the day's job sheets. 'Hang on. I'll check if I've got anything going up that way.' He mumbled the names of various towns to himself as he thumbed the paperwork. Mozzer became impatient.

'Don't worry about that, Baggy. I'll drive up.'

'No, don't be a prick. I might be able to kill two birds at once 'ere.' Mozzer realised yet again just how Baggy had become so successful. He never missed an opportunity to make money, or save it. 'Ere we go. I've got a drop in Lichfield. That'll do.'

'Lichfield! That's fuckin' miles away.'

'Mozzer, you are such a tit at times. It's up that way so it'll do. Now do you want the company, not to mention a driver, or not?'

His answer wasn't exactly that enthusiastic. 'Yeah, all right then.'

'Fuckin' hell. Thanks for making me feel wanted.'

Mozzer started to laugh as he realised the tone of his previous answer. 'Well, I only want to go to Nottingham, not on a tour of the whole bloody country.'

'Sod ya, then.'

'All right, don't get touchy.' He paused. 'What time do you want to do the off?'

'We can go as soon as, if you like. I'll just sort the van and be round in half an hour.'

'Yeah, all right, sounds good.' There was a short pause as a thought entered Mozzer's head. 'Have you got the delivery yet?'

'No, we'll pick it up on the way.' Baggy desperately tried to stop himself from laughing, but Mozzer could hear his muffled giggling.

'Oh, right-oh. Where the fuck's the pick-up?'

'Reading.'

'Oh, for fuck's sake, Ba . . .'

Baggy fell into fits of laughter and slammed the telephone down on his irate friend before he could let forth a torrent of abuse. Back in the privacy of his own home Mozzer stared at the dead telephone, then he also began laughing.

'He's such a wanker.'

Half an hour later Mozzer checked on the city outside his window. The two long blasts on the vehicle's hooter had indeed been Baggy's signal that he had arrived, and as usual he was too lazy to get out of his van and knock on the door. Mozzer grabbed the grey Calvin Klein zip-up jacket he had bought the previous day and headed out into the world. As the yellow Escort van headed out west on the M4, Mozzer told Baggy of the conversation he had had with his contact the day before.

'Well, it sounds to me that your man knows his stuff.'

There was a pause before Mozzer came back at Baggy.

'Yeah, does, don't it?'

Baggy realised that Mozzer's mind was running on overtime. He could almost see his brain ticking away inside his skull.

'You got a problem with this hit, ain't ya?'

'Kind of, yeah. Tell you the truth, I've got a few.'

'Like what?'

Mozzer turned to look at his driver's face in order to study any kind of reaction.

'I ain't told you this before, but you know my contact? Well, 'e's based in Nottingham.'

'Oh right. Well, that'll explain why he knows so much about this firm, won't it?' Baggy seemed unconcerned but knew his reaction was being scrutinised.

'Maybe.' Mozzer nodded his head and paused for a while. 'What about this, then. You know that police ID card Charlie lifted?'

'Yeah.'

'Well, that geezer was a Nottingham copper as well, weren't he?'

This time Baggy's reply was more thoughtful. 'Yeah.'

'Well, I think we might be getting set up.'

An unconvinced smile crossed the driver's face. 'What, just 'cos of that?'

Mozzer became both defensive and a little angry at his friend's dismissal of his hunch.

'Yeah. I think that's a bit iffy, even if you don't.' He shifted his body back so that he faced directly out of the front window.

'You've been watching too many cop programmes, you 'ave. Fuckin' hell, you wouldn't go out of your front door if you put two and two together like that every time.'

'Oh bollocks, to ya. I thought it was iffy, that's all.'

'Is that why we're going all the way to Nottingham? To check this pub is Kosher?' Mozzer remained silent and began to stare out of the passenger window. 'Fuck me.' Baggy's last two words were not going to go unchallenged.

'I suppose you got it right last Saturday then, did ya?'

Baggy continued to check the road ahead but his answer was definitely that of an unhappy man.

'Yeah, nice one, Mozzer. Cheers for that, mate.'

By the time they pulled off the M1 at junction 24 the atmosphere inside the van was back to the normal laughing and joking. Using the local *A to Z* Mozzer directed Baggy straight onto Sheriffs Way. The van moved slowly as the pair scoured the streets for the pub. Baggy quickly came up trumps.

'There she blows. The White Lion.' Both men studied the building as they drove slowly past. 'What a shit hole.' The pub was definitely not one of these new theme-type bars. This was a drinkers' pub, slightly run down and almost uninviting.

'Well, it looks the part, all right. Let's park up and then go check it out.' Baggy placed his right foot down a little harder on the accelerator and the van sped off in search of a resting place.

Ten minutes later they found themselves walking towards the front door of the pub. Both their stomachs were beginning to knot as they discussed the layout of the area.

'Good place for it, Mozzer.'

'I bet there's been a few good uns 'ere. Looks, well, naughty, don't it!' They walked on a few paces. 'Loads of places to do the off though.'

'Could be handy judging by what your mate said.'

Suddenly they were at the door.

''Ere goes.' The butterflies rose inside. It didn't matter that the match was still four days away, at times like this you could always bump into a face from the past and sometimes that could end up being nasty. Once inside, the pub provided a pleasant surprise. Although a little dark, the place was kept much cleaner than both had expected. Behind the bar stood a man in his late 40s, speaking to two punters propping up the other side. He straightened as Mozzer and Baggy walked across the room.

'What can I get you, lads?'

Mozzer turned to Baggy. 'What d'ya want?'

'Pineapple and lemonade, with ice.' He checked up on the bar menu as Mozzer added his own pint of lager to the order.

'You from London, lads?'

'Yeah. We're up 'ere working. Delivering stuff, you know?'

The barman turned to Baggy. 'You fancy some food, lad.? Our pies are top notch.'

Baggy remained fixed on the menu. 'What d'ya reckon, Mozzer. You hungry?'

'Yeah, why not?'

They placed their order then moved over to one of the tables by the window. Once out of earshot, Mozzer was the first to speak.

'Seems a bit too nice in 'ere for a footy firm to take over.'

'No, not really. You'd say the same about The George if you walked in there on a Tuesday, wouldn't' ya? Anyway it's what the beer and the food's like that matters.'

'Yeah, suppose so.' Mozzer nodded in the direction of the barman who was once again deep in conversation with his two old regulars. 'He don't strike me as the type to allow his pub to get smashed up though.'

''E's probably a homicidal maniac. The quiet ones are always the worst. 'E's probably put poison in our pies and sorting out with those two the best way to truss us up and shag us to death.'

'You're fuckin' weird, you are, Baggy. I don't know what Wendy sees in you when she could have a nice bloke like me.'

'She loves it, mate, always has.'

Some five minutes later the barman brought their food and laid it down on the table before them.

'There you go, lads. That'll be the best pie you'll get in Nottingham.'

Baggy's taste buds immediately sent messages to his brain. 'Cheers mate. Smells great.'

'Yeah, cheers, pal.' Mozzer took the chance to gain some information from their host. 'Big sporting city Nottingham, ain't it?'

'Oh yes.'

As Mozzer prepared to place the first forkful of food in his mouth he added another question.

'You a cricket or football fan?'

'Both, really. More cricket now, I suppose. Getting old, you see.'

Mozzer swallowed his food before continuing his interrogation. 'Do you get much trade from that?'

'Yeah, not bad. The cricket provides more than the football but being so close to the station helps us.'

'Yeah, course.' Mozzer had heard all he needed to hear.

Before the silence became embarrassing the barman made his excuses and left. The Londoners finished their food, enjoyed one more drink, then picked themselves up and left the pub.

As they walked back to the van Baggy asked Mozzer the big question. 'Well, how you feeling about it all now?'

'Better.' He paused and then began to explain his answer. 'If this firm are as new as matey says, and they are trying to keep it all quiet, then I reckon they could well use that place on Saturday, just as a one-off.'

'I think you're right. It's got to be a goer.' Both lads were in deep thought as they walked in the bright sunlight. 'It's a shame, really. That weren't a bad pie, and I quite liked that old boy.'

'What d'ya mean?'

'Well, we're going to smash the fuck out of his pub Saturday.'

You could almost hear the penny drop inside Mozzer's head. 'Oh yeah.' Then he became himself again. 'Ah, fuck him. Northern twat.'

58

Billy rose early the next morning. For him the best part of any stay in an English bed and breakfast was the early morning fry-up provided by an eager-to-impress host who, given the chance, could cook for England. Now he found himself out in the cool fresh air staring across the Bristol Channel thinking happily to himself. Billy already felt at home with Weston-Super-Mare. The holidaymakers passed him by, happily chatting to themselves or ordering their children to do this or that. He stood for half an hour just people-watching, but no one watched Billy and that was just how he liked it. Suddenly his thought process changed. He got himself together and headed off down along the front, thinking his plans through for the thousandth time.

He made his way into town in order to find himself a van-hire centre and within an hour he found himself sitting behind the steering wheel of the new red Escort van, a vehicle that was to become his property for the next seven days. It had been a long time since Billy had driven anything with four wheels and so he waited until the young lad had disappeared back inside the shop before trying to get to grips with the motor. His first attempt at moving off ended abruptly as the engine stalled, but panic failed to set in and soon all the old skills came flooding back and Billy headed off up the main drag. First stop was back at the bed and breakfast to pick up his jacket and the rest of his money. Billy settled the bill, checked his motorbike was still safe and locked up, and then went in search of a caravan site where he could hire a home for a few weeks. By midday Billy had everything in place. He felt good with himself. Once more he made his way back to town and parked up. Billy spent the next six hours walking the streets, eating and drinking in the cafés and enjoying a pint in what turned out to be a very friendly local. As he climbed back behind the wheel Billy smiled to himself. He nodded his head and spoke the words out loudly. 'Good shout, Billy. Like it.' He turned the key, pulled out from his space and directed the little red van back north towards Nottingham.

59

This time the venue for the briefing had changed. The officers involved in the operation needed to be clued up on their surroundings and so a visit to the White Lion pub was seen by DI Young as a must, although 8.30 a.m. on a Thursday morning was a little early for some of his men. He had left no stone unturned and had personally checked every folder to make sure his officers had the street and building plans they needed, as well as the photographs of their targets. The landlord was busy making sure that there was enough coffee and biscuits on show to keep his guests happy as the DI called order by tapping the side of his cup with his spoon. The room fell silent.

'Gentlemen, welcome. First let me introduce you to the gentleman running around at the back of the room doing his best to make us feel comfortable.' All eyes turned on the landlord whose cheeks suddenly reddened at being the focus of attention. 'This man is John Ramage, landlord of this establishment.' The officers muttered their hellos, a gesture acknowledged by the wave of a hand. 'Now I am sure you will appreciate that our host would like to keep his establishment looking just as it does now. Is that right, John?'

'Yes. Yes, I would, that's right.' The landlord hurried his answer, not wanting to take any further part in the proceedings. DI Young redirected his attention back towards his own men.

'You hear that. Now it is your job to ensure that our target on Saturday, the CBA, do not get within 50 yards of the front door of this building. Is that clear?' The room remained quiet. 'Right, if you open your folder you will find details of the part you will personally play during Saturday's operation. One very important detail you all need to keep firmly fixed in your minds is that the whole operation will be filmed. This film will, along with last week's footage, provide the main backbone of the evidence we need for any convictions. If you look at the street and pub plans, then you will see marked the positions of all the filming equipment.

'As you can see, we will have two cameras inside this building. One in here, and one upstairs. We will also have positioned two surveillance units. One will be positioned on Meadows Way, the other parked directly opposite the main entrance to this building. Now I have no doubt that some of you will have to use, shall we say, dubious tactics on Saturday. It is therefore important that you do not get yourself into a position where any such action will turn up on film for the defence lawyers to use against us. Is that clear?'

DI Young took a sip of water in order to clear his throat. He then continued the briefing.

'Supporting us on the day will be three units waiting in unmarked lorries. Each unit will consist of 20 uniformed officers. They will be led by radio directions. One unit will be parked up in Meadows Way. Another will be awaiting orders while parked up at the train station. The other will be placed in Robin Hood Way. That enables us to cover all the main routes into this area. When you read your orders you will find that the majority of you will be situated inside this building. Your role is to play the part of a typical football supporter-cum-hooligan. You will act in the manner of laddish supporters, some in here, some outside on the pavement.'

DI Young took a moment to steady himself and let the information sink in before moving on.

'We will also have two units placed in London, consisting of three officers each. One will be outside The George public house, where the CBA drink, the other at Kings Cross station. I hope that that way we will be able to get an early fix on their movements. If not, we should be able to pick them up on the motorway at some point.

'One other thing you need to be aware of. On Saturday this pub will, I repeat, *will* be open to the public.'

The statement brought an uncertain murmur from the assembled officers. A shout came from the back.

'Isn't that a little risky, sir?'

'Yes. Yes it is, Milton. That is why you need to keep the CBA away from entering this building.'

'Why don't we just shut it to the public?'

'Because we have to take into account that the CBA could possibly send forward what they call "scouts". These are hooligans who enter a "home" pub in order to check that their opposition is actually inside. Now if that does indeed happen then we need to make them think we are, in fact, the real thing. If they thought otherwise then they wouldn't bother hitting this place. Unfortunately, if the operation is to be successful, we have no choice.'

More muffled words filled the air. Detective Beck sparked up.

'Sir, if we have to look the real McCoy then we'll all have to be drinking.'

A loud cheer filled the room. DI Young raised his eyebrows,

followed by his hands with which he gestured to quieten down the room once more.

'Beck, I am sorry to disappoint you, but you will only be served with alcohol-free beer.' The answer was met with a chorus of jeers. 'The landlord, Mr Ramage, has been informed that all our men will only order one of two beers. One lager, one bitter. Whenever you order a round you must refer to the barman by name. That way they will know your pint is to be pulled from the correct, alcohol-free barrel.' He paused to let the moans die down, then smiled as he took a dig at Beck. 'Thank you for bringing that up though, Detective Beck. And I would like to ask you in particular not to drink too much of that either. We don't want you wetting yourself when the fun starts, do we?'

The rest of the officers joined in the ridicule of their colleague.

'Right, make yourselves familiar with all the details you have. The pub, the surrounding streets, etcetera. This will prove to be a very high profile operation once we pull it off. That will reflect well on all of us, so do your best and good luck.' He paused. 'And remember those camera positions.'

60

Pinhead was busy passing photocopies of the newspaper article around the pub. Thankfully The George hadn't suffered too much damage from the petrol bomb attack, and the windows had been replaced thanks to the whip-round money provided by the other lads during their Sunday afternoon drinking session. The police had been surprised that such a violent attack had taken place on the pub, a pub that, in their eyes, usually gave them very little trouble. The police, without the time or the resources, were happy to let the matter rest and had provided the landlord with the appropriate paperwork to claim for any damages from his insurance company, and so now the matter was closed.

Stokey had put in a show despite his injury from the previous week. The cut on his cheek drew special attention from the lads of the CBA. That would be a permanent reminder to them all of what in the end turned out to be a memorable day in their chequered history. Clive was not so lucky. He was still in his sick bed and nowhere near ready to rejoin the lads whose company he loved so much. As ever, Mozzer and Baggy were planning at their table in the far corner.

'If we're gonna do it we 'ave to be selective, Baggy. We can't take any chancers with us on this one.'

'Yeah, sure. Do the same as we did on the Yo-Yo Club. Just the top boys. If we go in tooled-up like we did there, then we'll fuck 'em over easy.'

'We better take a few more. I mean, my man said they'd have up to 50 lads.'

'All right. We take 30 lads, top whack. Remember, they ain't got a clue that we're coming. We'll hit that pub hard, full on, Mozzer. Do what Leeds did down 'ere. Petrol, CS gas, the fuckin' works.'

'Can you get CS gas?'

'Yeah, shouldn't be a problem. I tell you what, I'll take a Vick spray full of ammonia an' all. That's a fuckin' killer, that is.'

'Bleedin' hell, Baggy, what's got into you?'

'They took the piss coming in 'ere last week and dropping those cards. I think you'll find the rest of the lads feel the same way.'

Mozzer took a short look around the pub. As ever, it was buzzing. Everyone was expecting something to be planned for the Forest firm and so the anticipation in the air was electric. Mozzer continued the conversation. 'What do ya say we do this one in a hire van?'

'What, a seven an' a half tonne?'

'Yeah, that'll get 30 in the back easy.'

Baggy thought the plan through for a few seconds. 'Yeah, nice. I'll sort that. I'll get an unmarked one. I don't think we should pick up 'ere though, not after last week and that paper write-up.'

'Definitely not. We'll get the lads to make their own way up to Stanmore tube and pick 'em up there at about half ten, yeah?'

'Sweet. Now you go get the beers in an' I'll put the word round.'

'Remember, Baggy, only the top lads. And well tooled-up. And I mean, well tooled-up.'

61

Billy had had trouble sleeping during the night and so had got up as soon as the sun had flicked through the gap in his curtains. The anticipation and the excitement of the coming days had his mind spinning as he chose and carefully packed all that was dear to him. In truth, that didn't amount to much, as Billy Davis was not what you would call a collector. He had already packed what he could retrieve from his factory and so now it was down to what books, music and ornaments he wished to continue sharing his life with. From his porn collection he packed only those magazines with his favourite girls spread across the pages, as well as a few choice videos that had helped him pass away many boring afternoons. From the kitchen he took only the bare minimum. Two cups, a handful of cutlery, a few plates and some cooking utensils. The bigger items, such as the cooker and fridge, would have to stay. It didn't really matter to Billy as they were well old and needed replacing anyway. Billy felt warm inside as he made his decisions. He also felt nervous. Nervous at the thought of DI Young paying him an uninvited visit, and with that in mind Billy was desperately trying to keep the flat having that lived-in look about it. He was also nervous at the thought of making a brand new start, nervous and excited.

By midday Billy had all of the boxes he wanted piled up by the back door.

'Right, let's do it, Billy boy.'

First off, he went to the spare room. Billy opened the door and his eyes fell upon his prize possession. He dragged the small chest of drawers to the back door and then, using all his strength, lifted the unit and hobbled out to his hired Escort van. Billy opened the back and slid the unit as far down the van as it could possibly go. Quickly he filed up and down the path, adding box after box. He piled them in as if to protect the chest of drawers from prying eyes and thieving hands. Finally, he took a red petrol can from his outside cupboard and placed it on the floor by the passenger seat. Within 30 minutes the job was complete. Billy then grabbed his jacket and crash helmet before jumping into the van and heading back south to Weston-Super-Mare. As he hit the A453 the sun beat down and the temperature in the little van became unbearable. Billy wound down the window and the cool air brushed his face. He leaned forward and pressed the cassette into the player. The sound of REM filled his ears. Billy couldn't do *that* on his motorbike and he loved this special treat. His right arm rested out of the open window as a warm glow filled his body. Billy smiled and spoke to himself once more.

'Life ain't so bad, after all. And if I can pull this off, it's gonna get even better!'

The journey down took longer than Billy had expected. The Friday afternoon traffic of the M42 and M5 had obviously become topped up with people desperate to get away from work early so that they could make the most of the weekend and the glorious sunshine. Once he arrived at the coastal town, Billy turned left off the main drag and was pleased to be greeted by the sight of his GPZ sitting in front of him, the machine still safe and sound. He parked up and reached for the petrol can. Billy then climbed out of the van, went to his bike and tucked the can into his top box. He went back to the van, took his leather jacket and crash hat from the passenger seat and locked the vehicle. Billy walked around to the back and checked the doors. He did the same with the passenger doors and then the driver's door once more, just for safety. Billy then straddled his motorbike and started her up. He pulled on the skid lid and sat there for a while allowing the engine to warm up. For Billy, leaving the van unattended would be the worst part. His whole future lay within the metal panels of that van. If some spotty youth fancied a joy ride, or some petty villain wanted to check its contents, then Billy could lose everything. He took a deep breath.

'Well God, if ever you want to help, then help me now. Please.' He pulled in the clutch, flicked the engine into first gear and pulled away. It took all his strength not to take one final look back over his shoulder.

When Billy reached Junction 9 of the M5 he turned off and headed towards Evesham. He checked his mirror. Billy felt sure that no one was on his tail but a back route home would help to ease his mind. Billy soon found just what he wanted. As he pulled up to the queue of traffic, Billy looked over his shoulder. Pulling out he then gave the GPZ full throttle. If anyone had indeed been on his tail, now the chase was over. Billy was long gone. He headed off towards Redditch, where he stopped at the first garage he came to. He filled the tank of the motorbike, followed by the petrol can before heading into the shop and buying four large bottles of cheap lemonade. Within ten minutes the visit was over and Billy was back on his way home for the last time.

When he arrived back at the flat Billy was pleased to see that the place actually did still looked lived-in. Of course he would notice the odd missing item, but not the untrained eye. Thankfully the answerphone had not recorded any messages and there were no notes from DI Young to say that he or that prat Lopes had called. Billy made his way into the kitchen, placed the petrol can and the bag full of bottles on the sideboard and put the kettle on. As the water boiled, Billy poured the lemonade down the sink. He then used the bread knife to cut the top off the washing-up liquid bottle in order to produce a makeshift funnel. He poured the boiled water into the cup and waited for the tea to brew. Billy found himself drifting away, staring out of the window at nothing in particular, his mind full with way too many thoughts. As a small child ran by he shot Billy a glance that brought the Londoner back to life. He stirred the drink, removed the tea bag and carried on with the job in hand. The child had made Billy realise that he was standing in full view of the world outside, and so he took the empty bottles and his makeshift funnel into the now-vacant spare room. Billy returned to the kitchen, took four Jay cloths from under the sink, picked up his tea and the petrol can then made his way back to the room where the bottles were waiting.

One by one Billy filled them with petrol before lining them up against the wall. He stood looking at his handiwork then left the room, locking the door firmly behind him. Billy realised that the day had passed without him taking one decent meal, and so he limped off to the takeaway on the corner. He had thought of popping into the local for a goodbye drink, but in truth the people there meant nothing to him and so he soon found himself back home. Billy ate his vegetable curry without realising it, as his mind worked one stage ahead of his body. He washed the plates then made for the bathroom. Billy took a long hard look at himself, pulling all kinds of faces and making stupid remarks before finally reaching for the razors. At first the blades tugged at the hair, pulling the brown strands painfully from the skin. The first two blades soon became blunt under the intensity of their task, but the job became easier as he went on and Billy suddenly began to enjoy the emergence of his new look. His memory drew back the years, back to the days when he stood on the terrace as a spotty youth with hundreds of other shaven-headed lads.

'Skin . . .'ead.' He laughed at his own words as he continued with the transformation, the razors cutting away at the last few millimetres of stubble. The blade nicked his skin, forcing Billy to wince. He turned his head to view the cut and watched as the blood mixed itself with the water and shaving foam already on his scalp. The pink mixture quickly found a path down his neck and began dripping into the sink turning the colour of the water.

'Bastard thing.' Billy had learnt his lesson and took the last few scrapes of the blade a little more carefully. Once satisfied, he washed off the soap with warm water, then used cold to stop the flow of blood from the cut. He stood up straight and admired himself in the mirror.

'Billy, you should have done this years ago. That looks the dog's bollocks.' He paused for a while, his mind once again flashing back to days gone by. 'Davy would have been proud of ya!'

Billy had to check that one final item was still sitting safely in its place, before he tried to gain some much needed shut eye. He entered the front room, slid his hand under the upholstery of the chair and his fingers quickly found their prize. Tomorrow that gun would see the cold light of day for the first time in almost four years.

62

DI Young and Detective Lopes had already briefed the uniformed officers brought in just for the day. Young was more on edge than Lopes had ever seen him as he snapped at constables whom he felt asked too many questions. The uniformed officers were always like that, trying to get themselves noticed, or having ideas above their station. They wanted to know every detail, when in reality they were just bodies needed to swing the odds well and truly in the favour of the law. Lopes did his best to act calm and reassure his superior.

'Well, sir, this is it. I think you have everything covered.'

'Yes. I just hope one of the London units can pick up the CBA early on. That would make me feel a lot happier.'

'We'll pick them up at some stage. Remember, these are just mindless thugs, they'll cock it up somewhere along the way.'

DI Young had too many thoughts of his own buzzing around in his head to register Lopes' idle chit-chat. He checked his watch. 8.49 a.m.

'Right, we've got time for a quick coffee before meeting the rest of the unit. I want everyone in place by half past ten, and that includes us in the camera van opposite the pub.

63

Surprisingly, Billy had managed to get in a good seven hours' sleep. He felt excited, alive and totally in control. For the first time in as long as he could remember, Billy had gone without his early morning spliff. He couldn't afford to be sluggish in any way, as today he needed to be on the case from the moment he climbed out of bed. He went to work immediately. As Billy unscrewed the lids from the lemonade bottles the fumes from the petrol gave his head a bang. What a lovely smell that was, sweet, inviting. He stretched his eyes and slightly turned his head away so as to reduce the effect the vapours were having on him. Billy poured some of the leftover petrol from the can into a saucepan, then one by one he dipped the tips of the Jay cloths in the liquid and primed the weapons. Once ready he took the bottles out to his motorbike and placed them carefully in the top box, using scrunched up newspaper to hold them firmly in place and upright. Billy then retrieved the gun from its hiding place, checked the weapon over and tucked it inside the pocket of his motorbike jacket. As Billy took one last look around the flat he felt the adrenalin rise. He wasn't sorry to leave this place. He took hold of a tin of blue spray paint and went to work on the front-room wall. Again the room filled with intoxicating fumes as Billy carried out his work of art. Once finished, he stood back to admire his masterpiece. Billy beamed like a Cheshire cat then carefully placed the can on the floor in the middle of the room before leaving the flat through the back door. The GPZ was as reliable as ever, the engine firing at the first request. Billy was off to work. He never looked back.

Billy's first stop was to check on the White Lion pub. He rode past the building slowly, and was pleased to see that the location was quiet. He then headed off towards the police station where DI Young and Lopes were based. Billy's heart skipped a beat as he scooted past the back entrance of the cop shop. In the courtyard he spotted line after line of officers in uniform waiting to climb into the back of three white unmarked lorries. He had hit the jackpot. Also milling around were other coppers in plain clothes, talking, looking excited and leaning on yet more, but smaller, vans while enjoying a sneaky fag break. Billy spun the bike around and rode past the back entrance once more just to confirm his delight. Out of the corner of his eye he caught two men as they appeared from the building, one in casual gear, the other in the full regalia. They were DI Young and Lopes.

'Yes. Got ya, you bastards.' Billy moved off towards the end of the main drag and parked the bike. He climbed off the machine and waited, keeping the entrance in full view.

64

Mozzer had taken the tube to the end of the Northern line. He climbed the steps at Stanmore station and immediately saw the blue van opposite. He crossed the road to find that most of the lads were already sitting in place and Camden enjoying his first canned lager of the day. Mozzer shot a tame warning at the new boy.

'Oi. Not too much of that before we hit Nottingham. You'll need to be on it, not shit-faced.'

Camden removed the can from his lips, a look of embarrassment crossing his face. Mozzer then exchanged the usual greetings before moving around to the driver's cab. He found Baggy chomping away on a cold bacon sandwich. He banged hard on the driver's window, making Baggy jump. 'All right, geezer.' Pieces of half-chewed food fell from Baggy's mouth on to his clean Armani jeans.

Baggy opened the door. 'Prick, you scared the life out of me.'

'What, a big boy like you?'

They shared talk about their previous night's adventures before turning their attention to the day in hand.

'How you feelin'? Not still worried about the Old Bill, I hope?'

'No, it'll be sweet, I reckon.'

Despite the response, Baggy could tell that Mozzer was still a little troubled as his head shot from side to side, trying to pick out any prying eyes that the law might have fixed on them.

'The last place they will be looking for us is 'ere. By the way, look what I've got for us.' At last Mozzer focused his attention on Baggy as he undid the zip of a black and white Adidas holdall. 'Cop your eyes on this little lot, son.'

'Fuckin' hell, Baggy. Where'd you get all that?'

Baggy reached in the bag and pulled out one of the small CS gas sprays. 'Me mate Roger. He owns an army surplus warehouse. He gets offered this shit all the time apparently. You know me, I don't usually go for this kind of gear, so I'd never thought about it until last week. Result though, eh?' He handed the weapon over for Mozzer to study.

'Fuckin' right. How many have you got?'

'Forty.'

'How much was this little lot, then?'

'Fuck all, mate. I'll run him some gear around for nothing at some time.'

Mozzer stared, transfixed by the small cannister in his hand. 'How do ya use 'em?

'Don't ask me. Just point 'em, I suppose.' Baggy nodded his head towards the back of the van. 'Go try it out on Stokey. He knows what it feels like.' Both the lads started laughing.

'You're a cruel fucker, you are, Baggy.' Mozzer threw the small canister back in the bag. 'Better keep them out of sight for now. I'll take them in the back with us. What else you got?'

'Just the usual.' Baggy showed off his trusty two rings. 'You want to see what the rest have brought along though!'

'Yeah. Well, look I'll check everyone's here, an' if they are we better do the frank. I'll bang on the back of the cab when we're ready. All right?'

'Ah, ain't you gonna sit up here with me?' Baggy patted the passenger seat lovingly with the palm of his hand.

'Maybe later, love.' Mozzer winked at his friend then added in his best camp voice. 'You keep it warm though won't you, darlin'!'

He moved around towards the back of the van and rounded up the troops. When he was certain all were present and correct he ordered them to climb in and pulled down the shutter. He clambered over the mass of bodies and outstretched legs then banged on the metal panel that separated them from Baggy and his new driving companion,

Charlie. The motor shuddered into gear and the lads of the CBA felt the vehicle motion forward. As usual the journey north started with a song.

... 'ERE WE GO ... 'ERE WE GO ... 'ERE WE GO ...

65

Billy was jolted upright by the sudden movement from the back entrance of the police station. One by one the unmarked cars and lorries appeared and then pulled away. Once the flurry of activity had died down, Billy mounted the GPZ and made off towards the White Lion using an alternative route. Billy took his time over the short journey as he wanted to ensure that he could pick out the position of each individual lorry. Once he knew where they were all waiting it would help him to work out his own game plan. Pretty soon Billy had all the lorry locations sussed and had noticed that many of the officers in plain clothes had disembarked from their cars and made the final part of their journey on foot. Billy kept himself well hidden and close to his bike, a motorcycle magazine providing his face with a shield and helping to add realism to his presence at the same time. He felt the buzz rising inside. It had been many years now since he had become involved in such an event. The number of police involved in the operation had taken him by surprise, but after thinking things over he still felt that he had the means at his disposal to see things through. From his safe distance Billy watched the police unravel their plans, as officers came and went from the front entrance of the public house. He couldn't help but admire the efforts DI Young had gone to. At 10.46 on a Saturday morning the White Lion looked like any other pub. Innocent people went about their business, casually walking past, totally oblivious to what was unfolding around them. Billy wondered what those very same people would make of it if they just happened to be making the return journey in an hour or two's time. For their sakes, Billy hoped that they would be taking an alternative route home.

As Billy looked on, his hand fell on the cold metal of the weapon sitting in his jacket pocket. His memory shot back to the day when he took revenge on his hit-and-run driver and he became lost for a moment. Suddenly Billy felt as if a bolt of electricity had shot through him. His mind jolted back into action, focused. From the front entrance, Detective Lopes came into view. This was the final piece of the jigsaw as far as he was concerned. At last he had spotted the location of his ultimate target. His finger clutched at the handle of the gun.

'Lopes, I've got you.' He watched as his target crossed the road and climbed into the back of the white Transit parked directly opposite the pub entrance. Again, whispered words came from Billy's lips. 'So, that's where you're hiding!' He smiled and began to laugh inside. 'Stay there monkey and you're dead meat. Picking you off will be easier than I thought.'

66

Mozzer banged hard on the metal panel desperate to gain Baggy's attention.

'BAGGY, WHERE THE FUCK ARE WE?'

Initially the noise had made the driver swerve, sending his passengers banging into each other. Baggy turned to Charlie.

'Prat. That's twice he's scared the shit out of me this morning. Check the map out for me and tell him where we are.'

It had been agreed by the two main men that it would be best to take a back route rather than the motorway. The idea being that they would enter Nottingham from the east on the A52 rather than from the west and the motorway that way they should get in undetected. Charlie soon found their location and shouted the information back to Mozzer.

'WE'RE JUST PAST CORBY. WHY, YOU WANT A PISS STOP?'

'YEAH. PULL OVER WHEN YOU GET THE CHANCE. BUT MAKE SURE IT'S SOMEWHERE QUIET.'

Within minutes Mozzer felt the van turn and ride over some rougher ground. Rod tugged at the shutter and daylight came into view for the first time in over an hour. The lads jumped out, began to stretch their legs and took a much needed leak. Mozzer took the chance for a chat with his driver.

'Bloody hell, that's rough in the back there.' He rubbed his arse.

'I told you to bring something soft to sit on.'

'I ain't bringing a cushion to bloody football, you tart.'

'Well, stop fuckin' moaning, then. Look, we got about the same again to do. I don't want to stop again, I think you should jump in the front with me. Charlie won't mind, he'll go in the back.'

'There's room for another one as well, ain't there?'

'Yeah, get Danny up front as well.'

Mozzer headed off to sort out his troops. Once the seating arrangements had been made he offered out the CS gas sprays. Ten minutes later the CBA were once again heading north, every passing minute getting closer to the enemy. Baggy tried to sound upbeat as he broke the silence in the driver's cab.

'How ya feeling, Mozzer?'

'Tell you the truth, I am shitting myself.' Once again silence descended.

67

The prying eyes of Detective Alan Lopes were searching out the area as DI Young sat watching the two television screens that sat in the racking at the back of the surveillance van. The addition of the two men had made space short, as the usual three occupants did their best to go about their business. Lopes watched his colleagues as they drank outside the White Lion. He wished that he could be out there with them but his governor had denied him that opportunity by insisting that he stay hidden in the van. At this delicate stage DI Young didn't want Lopes's ugly mug to get recognised and so he had taken away the understudy's chance to smash a few Cockney faces. DI Young continually tried to convince himself that every angle had been covered.

'Um, yes. That is a good view. Clear.' He checked his watch. 11.58 a.m. 'Well, it looks like we will have to rely on our men up by the motorway. We should have picked them up by now, surely.' He ordered one of the other officers present to call his spotters up at the station, in the hope that they could throw some light on the whereabouts of the CBA. The answer was not the one he had hoped for.

'Sorry, sir, they have nothing to report as yet.'

'Shit. Where the hell are they?'

Lopes offered up some kind of reassurance. 'Don't worry, sir. They won't get anywhere near this pub without us spotting them first. Not in a million years.'

DI Young let the comment pass over him as his head continued to spin. 'Could be any time now, any time.' He turned to his understudy. 'Seen anything yet, Lopes?'

'No. Not really.'

DI Young was looking for anything to ease the tension rising in his body. 'What do you mean "not really"?'

'Well, I've been watching that guy right over there. The bloke with the motorbike.'

Young got to his feet, the other occupants of the van also beginning to take an interest.

'What guy?'

Lopes pointed out the shaven-headed biker in the distance to his superior. Young watched him for a moment.

'Oh, he's nothing.'

Lopes continued his fix on the man. 'Well, you never know. He might be "scouting" the place.'

'I doubt it. He's too far away, too obvious and on his own.'

'Do you want me to get a man over there and have a word, just to make sure?'

The question made DI Young snap.

'For Christ's sake, Alan, forget it. Anyway if he were a "scout" then sending an officer over would blow the whole thing wouldn't it! Think things through before you make a suggestion, will you?'

Lopes gave up on the idea and came away from his vantage point.

68

Inside Billy was racing. Suddenly he wasn't so sure whether his plans would work or not. What would happen if Mozzer and the CBA failed to show? What would happen if he failed to get to Mozzer in time? What if his motorbike let him down, or he was sent skidding off? If only he had a joint to calm his nerves. If only. He studied every passing vehicle and clocked all the comings and goings of the pub. Billy fixed his eyes on the vehicle that held Lopes deep inside and wondered what was going through the mind of his prize. He became more and more agitated, impatient.

'Come on, Mozzer. Come on.'

69

As the van approached Bingham, Baggy hung a left and turned off the A46. He tried his best to calm the nerves that were building up inside of him

'Not far now, lads.'

Mozzer offered up a plan. 'What do ya reckon we do a drive past the pub, see how things are shaping up?'

Danny agreed.

'Yeah, good shout. We might get an idea of what we're up

against before we park up and do the business. Bosch.'

Baggy sealed the deal, giving the plan his personal nod of approval. 'I am up for that. They won't know who the fuck we are. We can suss out what the score is with the Old Bill at the same time. I mean if they're crawling all over the joint then all bets off from the start anyway.'

As they entered the outskirts of Nottingham, Mozzer banged on the panel behind him and warned the lads to get ready as the battle was just minutes away. The buzz was now really kicking in.

Danny couldn't keep his thoughts to himself. 'I am fuckin' looking forward to this.' The aggression began to rise in his voice as he became more and more wound up. 'We'll teach these wankers not to come down and play Mickey Mouse with us on our patch.'

Baggy joined the conversation. 'Dropping posters in the lav'. That's fuckin' 'ard that is, well 'ard.'

Mozzer was lost in the middle as the two began to boil. Danny added to the atmosphere.

'We're gonna sort this lot before they've even started. They won't come on our turf again. No fuckin' way. Never.' He pulled the cosh from his pocket and began to bounce the lead ball off his thigh. At the sight of the weapon Mozzer automatically went for his own baby. The knuckle-duster slid gently into position. The fingers of his right fist closed around the handle, gripping it tightly.

'There she is.' Mozzer began to rub the steel into the palm of his left hand. It felt cold, smooth. The slow rubbing motion made him feel calm, comforted. Slowly he rubbed. The words he spoke were quiet. 'Come on. Come on. Let's go to work.' Each one of them was in a world of their own, and the van was within a mile of the White Lion pub.

Baggy turned off London Road and drove the van slowly past the train station. The area was already awash with football fans and police.

'Bloody hell, my contact was right. He said steer clear of the station.'

Danny stretched his neck for a better view. 'The coppers look like they're expecting something, there's hundreds of the bastards.'

Baggy moved the van on before turning into Sheriffs Way. ''Ere goes. It's just down here.'

As they turned the bend the pub shot into view and the three lads caught their first sight of the lads standing outside drinking. Mozzer was first to speak and he couldn't hide the surprise in his voice.

'Well, fuck me, the old contact has come up trumps again.' He turned to face his driver. 'Baggy, son, I swallow. All that worrying about the Old Bill. Sorry, mate.'

Baggy sounded nervous. 'Yeah, they look the real deal to me all right.'

As the van drew level with the front door Mozzer got a better idea of the task about to face his firm. 'Jesus. They ain't half got some boys in there. Got to be 60, 70 at least.'

Danny was more excited. His head shook from side to side as his excitement grew. 'Oh, we're gonna do these cunts, no worries.'

All worries of a police set-up had now left Mozzer, and he was also buzzing at the thought of going into battle against such a large mob. He slapped his hand down on Danny's shoulder.

'This is gonna be lovely.'

Baggy gave the van a little more juice. 'Right, let's get parked up.'

70

Billy was quick to notice the blue van heading towards him, the head movement of the driver and his passengers as they all checked on the White Lion drawing special attention. He focused his eyes the best he could on the man at the wheel as the van drew level.

'Fuck me, that's Baggy.' Billy immediately recognised the driver as the man he had stood shoulder to shoulder with during many terrace battles. He threw his paper to the ground and swung his leg over the seat of his GPZ. As quick as he could, he pulled on the crash hat and fired the engine. He couldn't risk losing sight of his old friend. Billy tried to pull away as innocently as possible, but in his hurry the back wheel flicked off to the left, letting forward the screech of spinning rubber.

The cry of the burning tyre had not been lost on Detective Lopes.

'Sir, that biker. He's just shot off. But really sudden, like.'

DI Young got to his feet and joined his underling at the spy hole.

'Why, what happenned?'

'I don't know, but he seemed to head off after some blue van.' He paused for a moment then turned to his superior. 'I wonder if that's them. It's well possible they could be piled up in the back of one those.'

DI Young took just a split second then headed for the radio.

'All units. All units. Our target may be in the area. Watch for a large blue van and a motorbike.'

He repeated the message once more then returned to join Lopes, the buzz now also raging within both of them.

71

'This'll do, Baggy, hang a right 'ere.' Baggy did as Mozzer asked and steered the vehicle into Robin Hood Way. The orders continued. 'There, perfect. Park up down here somewhere.' After a few hundred yards Baggy pulled in and switched off the engine.

Danny jumped out, ran around the back and lifted the metal shutter. 'This is it, lads. Lets fuckin' do it.'

The lads of the CBA poured out onto the street. Shep, Camden, Clarkie. In all they totalled 32, all the top boys, and all desperate to get stuck in to the Forest firm.

The driver of the white lorry watched in his wing mirror as Mozzer and Baggy headed up the road towards him, their troops surrounding them. Slowly he sank down in his seat in an attempt to avoid getting sussed. He watched as the Londoners grew in number and buoyed each other up for the violence that lay just around the corner. His body began to sweat as their numbers grew and they displayed their armoury of weapons. Baseball bats, pool cues. Golf and snooker balls. The policeman wanted desperately to reach for the radio and give out a warning but he daren't. All he could do for now was sit it out and watch. He heard a slight noise from the back of his truck and his heart jumped. He prayed for all he was worth that his cargo of policemen would remain silent as even the slightest noise would give the game away. Suddenly the mob began to move forward. Everyone of them looked alert, fired up. They spread across the road, their numbers appearing to double into a violent heaving mass, eager to hunt out their enemy. At last it was safe. He grabbed for the radio.

'All units. I have the target in view. They are presently in Robin Hood Way and are moving off in the direction of the White Lion.'

DI Young snatched the microphone from its resting place.

'DI Young here. How many suspects do we have?'

The voice crackled back. 'Approximately 30, 40 maybe. All have weapons. Lots of weapons. Over.'

The head policeman gave out his final order.

'All units. Hold positions. Uniformed units, do not move until you have received the order. Repeat, do not move. This is it, gentlemen, get ready. Over.'

72

Somehow Billy Davis had lost sight of the blue van and the GPZ he was riding shot past the turning Baggy had taken just moments before. He cursed himself as he followed the road around a sharp left bend.

'*You fuckin' idiot.*' His mind raced. If he cocked up now then his plans would be blown. He decided to head back towards the pub. Showing little concern for his fellow motorists, Billy swung the Kawasaki around, forcing the driver behind to slam down hard on his brakes. The car's horn blasted loud at Billy who returned the anger with a display of his middle finger. As Billy glided the GPZ once more around the bend he twisted hard on the throttle and the machine let forth a powerful growl.

Almost half of the officers stationed up at the White Lion left the bar and headed for the street as requested during the morning's briefing. Detective Beck led the exodus. He had been counting the minutes in the build-up to this moment, and now his chance had arrived. For Beck, this was the opportunity for some lawful beatings to be dished out. Suddenly the lads of the CBA came into view. Instantly the hairs on Beck's neck rose. He became nervous. The detective had watched the video footage over and over. He had convinced himself that these lads were nothing more than idiots, and had told his fellow officers that the Londoners were cowards, only brave when the numbers were heavily in their favour. But now his mind was giving forward other signals, signals of danger. He looked around to check the reaction of his fellow officers. Suddenly they too looked on edge. For the first time he noticed how old some of his colleagues were, too old for this kind of game. Old and out of shape. Detective Beck turned his eyes back on the mob closing in on the pub. He took one step back, realising his legs were beginning to shake as he went.

73

DI Young and Lopes watched as the firm from London moved closer. Without realising, Lopes spoke out loudly the names of the men they were hoping to trap, as one by one they came into view.

DI Young was constantly talking into his microphone. He held the mouthpiece close to his lips. 'Nobody move. Nobody move.' He tried his best to sound calm but the tone of his voice gave away the excitement that was welling up inside. 'We must draw them forward. We need them to be active before we strike. Beware of the camera positions and wait for my order.'

Lopes watched the scene unfold. The Londoners were moving closer by the second as his fellow officers spilled from the pub and spread themselves across the road. The adrenalin was pumping through his veins. 'This is unbelievable. Bloody unbelievable.' He turned to the surveillance team. 'Are we getting all this?'

The comment drew a sharp response. These men had seen it all many times before and they didn't need Lopes in the van, let alone on their backs.

'Yes. Of course we are.'

Suddenly a cry went up as the CBA came to a halt some 50 yards from the front of the pub. They baited what they thought to be the Forest hard-core.

. . . WE ARE EVIL . . . WE ARE EVIL . . .

Mozzer and Baggy wanted to draw the Nottingham lads out. They wanted the northern firm to unload their bottles and pint glasses before steaming forward themselves and using their own armoury to full effect. As the stand-off unfolded, Billy Davis came racing up the road behind the London firm and was forced to mount the pavement in order to get to Mozzer, his main man. Rod took a kick at the biker as he forced the machine past, but Billy felt nothing other than a dull thud on his thigh. He gave the GPZ another tug on the throttle before banging down hard on the brake and coming to a stop in no man's land.

The unexpected arrival of the biker had stunned everyone. Lopes turned to his boss. He couldn't hide his anger as the words shot out. 'It's that biker again. I told you he was one of them. I fuckin' told you.' He flashed his eyes back to the scene outside.

Mozzer was jolted backwards by the sudden appearance of the man dressed in black leather. Then he moved forward.

'DO THE CUNT.'

The top boy moved in on Billy, the metal on his right fist ready to smash its way through the gap of the helmet and hard into the biker's face.

Billy shouted as loud as he could.

'LONDON NO. NO. REMEMBER DAVY PHILIPS.'

The words hit Mozzer head-on. Immediately he shot his arms out sideways as a signal for the rest of his troops to stop. He screwed his eyes, desperately trying to work out just who had shouted the name of his dead friend. He took two steps closer.

'What did you say?'

The mob surrounded the biker, all thoughts of the Forest firm long gone from their minds. Billy shouted for all to hear.

'LISTEN TO ME. I AM YOUR CONTACT. DAVY PHILIPS'S MATE.'

Mozzer recognised the voice straight away but had trouble believing the sound in his own ears. Billy desperately tried to convince the Londoner.

'Mozzer, I set you up with Leeds at Crewe, didn't I?'

'Fuck me, it is.' Time seemed to stand still as Mozzer's brain tried to work the situation out he had suddenly found himself in. Baggy came to Mozzer's side and butted in.

'Who the fuck are ya?'

Billy lifted the front of the helmet so that the chin guard was resting on his forehead. He turned to his old fighting partner. 'It's me, Baggy. Billy. Billy Davis.' Baggy was stunned at hearing his own name, then the image of the face clicked in.

'No, it never is?' Sitting on the bike before him was his long-lost friend. The sudden realisation brought a smile to his face and he moved forward to greet Billy. 'What the fuck's going on? Where the fuck 'ave you bee' . . .'

Billy cut him short. He shouted the words for all the lads to hear. 'YOU'RE BEING SET UP. THIS LOT ARE ALL OLD BILL, GET THE FUCK OUT OF 'ERE.'

At first the words failed to register with Mozzer. 'No, you've got it wrong, pal. We're doin' the pub.'

'I tell ya. That lot are all filth, every one of 'em.'

Mozzer turned to face the coppers decked out in plain clothing. 'No, it can't be. Fuckin' bastards. I knew something was wrong with this.' He was annoyed at himself for finally being sucked in.

Up the road in the surveillance van DI Young began to panic as he began to lose control of his operation. 'WHAT THE HELL IS HAPPENING?' He shouted into his radio. 'DRAW THEM FORWARD. FOR CHRIST'S SAKE, SOMEONE DO SOMETHING.'

Detective Drummond took the order and launched the first pint glass at the mob of Londoners. The beer flowed from its container as the weapon spun through the air before crashing against the tarmac inches from where Mozzer was standing. More followed as the police set about their task. Soon the air was full of flying bottles, then the sound of breaking glass took over.

Baggy tugged at Mozzer's arm. 'We better do as Billy says. Let's get the hell out of 'ere.' They're trying to pull us on.'

Mozzer couldn't break his stare as the filth began to give it the large one. Slowly he began to retreat.

'It can't be Old Bill. No way.'

The firm slowly moved back, dodging the flying glass as they went. Billy Davis turned on his seat and reached into the top box of his motorbike. He removed two of the petrol bombs he had so lovingly prepared the night before, then produced a lighter from his pocket. He rested one bottle between his legs before setting light to the Jay cloth that was tucked into the top of the one he was holding. Billy wasted no time in disposing of his weapon. The bottle smashed onto the road and spread its flames among the advancing policemen. The filth were sent running for cover, some caught by the burning fuel. Mozzer, Baggy and the rest of the CBA stopped in their tracks, transfixed by the scene. Screams filled the air as a thick grey cloud rose skywards. Billy quickly sparked up the second weapon. In an instant that too was spreading its yellow and orange flames, drawing a hot impenetrable barrier between the two groups and blocking the entrance of the pub. Billy turned to see Mozzer and the firm. Again he shouted at the top of his voice.

'GET THE FUCK OUT.'

At last the words appeared to hit home. The lads of the CBA had seen enough and were on their toes. Billy grabbed one more bomb from the top box. He lit the fuse then placed the bottle between his legs before flicking the Kawasaki into gear. The biker then manoeuvred the bike into position and pulled on the throttle. He shouted the words as loudly as he could.

'THIS ONE'S FOR YOU, LOPES, YOU BASTARD.'

Billy rode the GPZ towards the unmarked van. The Kawasaki cut through the flames only to find the other side of the battleground in total chaos. Billy smashed the bomb down hard on the tarmac so that the fire engulfed the van.

Inside DI Young and the other officers heard the bang. Lopes jumped to his feet.

'What the hell was that?' Panic crossed his face.

DI Young continued to shout into his radio. 'WHAT THE HELL IS GOING ON?'

Billy snatched for the last bottle. Out of the corner of his eye he could see the officer closing in on him. There was no time in which to spark the weapon. He aimed the bottle at the advancing officer. Billy's direction was sharp, the bottle shattering down in front of his challenger. Most of the liquid splashed up, drenching the policeman. The soaking stopped the officer dead in his tracks, as the realisation that he was now primed shook through his body. The rest of the liquid spread itself across the road surface, reaching out, reaching further until it found its target. Then the fuel ignited. The sudden bang shut out all other sound, before the screams cut through. Billy sat mesmerised as the man before him transformed into a burning inferno. He reached inside his jacket and drew the revolver, the gun catching daylight for the first time. His finger pulled at the trigger and the weapon shook his hand. The torched body fell to the ground, dead.

In the van, Lopes shuddered at the crack of the weapon.

'I want out of here now.' He made for the door handle but DI Young gripped his hand. 'Stay there, Lopes. You're not going to fuck my operation, you hear?'

'Fuck you, SIR.' Lopes tugged his hand away and made for the exit.

Billy turned and screamed at the top of his voice before unloading the rest of the bullets in the direction of the surveillance van.

'LOPES, YOU BASTARD.' The weapon cracked once, twice, three times. That was enough. Billy dropped the gun then kicked the bike into action. Once again he cut a path through the mayhem. As he made his escape, Billy felt a kick in his back as Lopes and Young's hiding place exploded into the sky, taking the occupants with it.

The ripping noise of the explosion shook through every Londoner's body and the firm ran faster, not daring to look back. As they reached the turning of Robin Hood Way they came face to face with the unit of policemen as they spilled from the back of their lorry. The grabbing hands of the law snatched at the Londoners. The City lads fought back, their actions driven more by fear than anything else. The police were left helpless as Pinhead, Danny and the lads went to work with baseball bats, coshes and pool cues. Wood smashed against bone, cracked skulls, ripped-open flesh, and blood spilled from mouths, noses, heads.

Baggy headed straight for the driver's cab and fired up the engine. Charlie lifted the back shutter and was screaming for the lads to join him. One by one they climbed aboard as the coppers fell around them, or ran for all their worth. As the lads jumped into the safety of the van the air became full with the mist of CS gas. As Baggy pulled the vehicle from its resting place, Mozzer ran around to the back and slammed down the shutter before returning to join his number two up front.

'GO, BAGGY. FOR FUCK'S SAKE, GO.' The words were full of panic and excitement.

Baggy filled the air with an insane laugh as the ultimate rush rippled through his body. 'YEE HA! FUCKIN' HELL.'

Not one sentence made sense as the van sped away as fast as it could out of Nottingham, unaware of the true devastation they and Billy had left behind.

74

The police had made no fix on the vehicle and so, without making so much as one stop, Baggy drove straight back to a lock-up in Romford and parked the van. Once within the safety of the yard, Mozzer released the catch on the shutter and the lads of the CBA spilled out. The floor became awash with the urine that they had so desperately been holding in for the last two hours and their excited talk filled the air.

Mozzer turned to Baggy. 'We better get away from here. What's the time?'

The right-hand man checked his watch. 'Quarter to three.'

Mozzer thought for a while then the buzz rushed through him once more. He turned to his troops.

'Oi, lads, the day's just beginning. Palace are at home, ain't they? So who's up for a row south of the river?'

75

At 4.35 p.m. both the front and back doors were simultaneously sent crashing from their hinges. Within seconds 20 armed officers filled the small ground-floor flat and the disorientating tactics provided by the banging of shields and whistles quickly died down. Just one minute had passed since the start of the raid when, to the disappointment of the detective in charge, the building was declared empty.

An officer from the armed unit appeared and summoned Detective Beck forward.

'Sir, I think you should see this.'

He led his colleague through the hallway and into the front room. As Beck entered, his eyes fell upon the words sprayed across the wall in thick blue paint.

CONGRATULATIONS OLD BILL
YOU'VE JUST MET THE CBA
NOW FUCK OFF.

76

Billy Davis had wasted no time in getting back to the coastal town he had quickly grown to love. Once again, the Londoner had swapped his motorbike for the little red Escort that had kept his life savings and future plans safely hidden within its metal walls. He had then headed out to the holiday park and collected the keys for the mobile home which was to become his rest hole for the next few weeks.

For the first time Billy sat down to gather his thoughts. He breathed a huge sigh of relief as a calmness washed over him and his body felt the first groan of tiredness. Images flashed into view. First Mozzer, then Baggy. Billy remembered the burning policeman, closed his eyes and asked for forgiveness. That death was never meant to happen. A stab of hatred entered his brain as he thought of Lopes, but the pain was relieved as once again he lived out the thud from the exploding van. Billy smiled. The Londoner got to his feet, put the kettle on and then took up residence at the open door. He gazed out across the holiday park. Car after car loaded with people arrived, eager to enjoy their week in the sun. Once again, they all failed to notice Billy Davis. The Londoner moved back inside, closed the door behind himself and rolled a huge joint to go with his freshly brewed cuppa.

Billy enjoyed the silence for a while, but his mind soon began to play tricks with him. Burning images shot into focus and he quickly became uncomfortable with himself. To break the silence Billy pressed the button on the radio. The last occupant had left the volume on full, and the noise shook Billy rigid. He spun the dial to kill the intrusive sound.

'Fuckin' hell.' Billy checked his watch, it read 4.58 p.m. 'Shit, the football results.' He re-tuned the radio just as the voice gave out the good news.

'Forest 1. City 3.'

Billy punched the air. 'Yes. Go on, my son.'

77

In a pub just south of the River Thames the 3–1 win was greeted with the same reaction by Mozzer and the lads of the CBA. The main man turned to Baggy.

'RESULT.' He slapped Baggy's back. 'Right, let's get the lads, head up to Victoria station and go fuck Palace over.'

Baggy downed the last drops of his pint, slammed the glass on the table and took the challenge.

'Sweet, Mozzer. Let's fuckin' do it.'